The First Form Pr[...] the biggest events of t[...] a tradition since White Oak was founded – more than one hundred years ago. The Prom Princess is always a First Form student, and she is supposed to be the ideal White Oak girl. Being voted Prom Princess at the Spring Prom is a *huge* honour.

You might think it's weird that an all-girls boarding school has a prom, Diary. But boys from the nearby Harrington School for Boys take classes with us, and there are often shared activities between the two schools. The Prom Princess's date gets to be Harrington's Prom Prince!

"Are *all* these girls going to run?" I asked.

"I'm not," Jolene said. "I don't want to have to get all those signatures." She handed me a copy of the rules.

"The two girls with the most signatures by noon on Sunday will be the finalists," Holly Welsh explained.

I nodded and read the rules. Each White Oak student could nominate one – and *only* one – First Form girl. You nominated a girl by signing your name on her form. Once the two finalists were chosen, they had six days to try to convince students to vote for them. Each finalist would make a speech at an assembly for the whole school. Then everyone would vote at the dance the following Saturday. The winner would be crowned Prom Princess and become part of White Oak history.

"I'm with you, Jolene," Holly said. "I'd be scared to ask for signatures. What if everyone turned me down?" She shuddered.

"I have too much homework to run for Prom Princess," Banner Whist said. "I have a huge test in two days."

"I'll be much too busy with the video," I said.

"Me too," added Phoebe. She waved at our friends Cheryl Miller, Summer Sorenson and Elise Van Hook to come over. They had just come into the Student Union.

"What's up?" Summer asked.

I held up the nomination form. "It's Prom Princess time!"

Elise's eyes widened. "If all these girls are running for Prom Princess, there won't be anyone left to vote!"

"I don't think they're all running," I said.

"How many signatures do I need to win?" Marsha Avery asked.

"More than the rest of us," Natalie Pittman joked.

"Are you definitely running, Natalie?" Holly asked. "Because if you are, I have to decide whose form to sign – yours or Lavender Duncan's."

"What about mine, Holly?" Marsha asked.

"Well, uh . . ." Holly shrugged. "I'm not going to sign anyone's right now, Marsha."

"I'm running for sure," Natalie said firmly. She turned towards the door. "But right now I've got to run to softball tryouts!" She quickly left the Student Union.

"Uh, I have to go, too," Holly said. I could tell she felt uncomfortable. She wanted to get away from Marsha. Marsha frowned but didn't say anything.

Wow. This contest could get pretty serious, I realised. *A lot of girls will have to choose one friend over another for the first round of voting.*

And that's when I got the best idea!

I pulled Phoebe aside. "I have a topic for our video."

Phoebe grinned. "What is it?"

"Let's make a video about the Prom Princess contest," I said. "It's got drama, excitement *and* suspense. All the things Mr. Shanks said a good movie should have."

"I love it!" Phoebe exclaimed. We high-fived.

So that's what we're going to do, Diary. I just hope a film about a Prom Princess contest will be good enough to enter in the New Hampshire Film Festival!

Fingers crossed!

Dear Diary,

I'm sitting in bed and I'm having a hard time staying awake to write! Softball tryouts were today. I'm tired, thrilled and terrified!

Maybe I'd better explain that, Diary.

I'm tired because Coach Hadley worked the team really hard this afternoon. Each of us played more than one position, batted several times, and ran laps around the field. You can see why I'm so tired!

Now here's why I'm thrilled: I have a chance to break White Oak's home-run record.

Nine years ago, a girl named Jamie Jerome hit ten homers in twelve games. She was in Second Form – a grade ahead of the one I'm in. Well, I want to hit *eleven* home runs this season while I'm in *First* Form.

Ashley has known all winter about my plan. I told my roommate, Campbell Smith, today while we were waiting for tryouts to start. We were standing outside the dugout because the bench inside was full.

"You'll have to hit a home run every game, Mary-Kate," Campbell said, her brown eyes very serious.

"*Almost* every game," I corrected her. "There are twelve games in a season, but I only need eleven to beat Jamie Jerome's record."

"No problem," Campbell grinned. "If anyone at White Oak can do it, you can."

"Do what?" Dana Woletsky asked as she came up behind us. I noticed her cashmere sweater matched her green eyes and her brown corduroy miniskirt matched her hair. She was carrying a notebook.

Why is Dana here? I wondered. I knew it couldn't be good. Dana never misses a chance to make my life miserable.

"Mary-Kate wants to break – " Campbell started to answer Dana's question.

I cut her off. "Are you trying out for the team, Dana?" I didn't want anyone to know about my secret goal – especially Dana!

"I'm covering the softball season for the *Acorn*," Dana explained. The *White Oak Acorn* is the school newspaper. Dana is one of its editors.

"That's nice," I said. I don't like Dana, but I try not to be rude. It's not easy, Diary!

"So what are you going to break, Mary-Kate?" Dana asked again.

"Jamie Jerome's home-run record," Natalie Pittman said as she stepped out of the dugout. She must have heard Campbell and me talking.

"Great. I'll put that in my newspaper story," Dana said. She flipped open her notebook and started taking notes.

Oh, no! I stared at Dana. *Now* everyone *will know I'm trying to break the school home-run record. Talk about pressure!*

Coach Hadley blew her whistle to start the practice. She divided the players into two groups. One group ran onto the field. Campbell and I were in the first group to bat.

I love stepping up to the plate. I'm small, but I've got a good eye and a strong swing. I can usually tune out everything except the ball.

Today all I could feel was Dana staring at me.

Rachel Delmar's first pitch was right over the plate. I swung – and missed!

"What? Mary-Kate missed?" Dana exclaimed, surprised. "Now *that's* news!" She scribbled something in her notebook.

"Don't worry about it, Mary-Kate," Campbell called.

I took a deep breath and tightened my grip on the bat. I couldn't let Dana psych me out. I swung at the next pitch and hit a grounder.

"What kind of lame hit was *that*, Mary-Kate?" Dana yelled as I ran to first base. I stopped and glared at her.

"I don't think Jamie Jerome has to worry about anyone breaking her home-run record *this* year," Dana called across the field.

So that's why I'm terrified: Dana is going to blab it all over school that I'm trying to beat the record.

And I have no idea if I can!

Chapter 2

Thursday

Dear Diary,

Ashley and I sat together at lunch. My sister had to present her Prom Princess video idea to Mr. Shanks later today.

"So far only Marsha Avery, Lavender Duncan and Natalie Pittman are entering the contest," Ashley said.

"Only three?" I asked, surprised.

"A lot of girls are worried about competing," Ashley explained.

"Competition won't bother Natalie," I said. "I've seen her play basketball and softball!"

Ashley nodded. "I think Natalie likes to compete almost as much as she likes to win." She crumpled her juice carton. "How did tryouts go?"

"Okay, I guess," I said, frowning.

I didn't want to admit that Dana's taunts had thrown me off my game, but I share everything with Ashley. She would know that something was bothering me.

"Dana found out that I want to break the school home-run record," I explained. "She's going to write about it in the *Acorn*. Now everyone will know."

"That might not be so bad," Ashley said. "Everyone will be cheering you on."

"Everyone except Dana Woletsky," I said. "She can't wait to tell the whole school that I can't break the record."

"But you can!" Ashley said. "You're the best hitter on the team."

I smiled. My sister totally believes in me, Diary. It feels great!

"I'll catch you later, Mary-Kate." Ashley stood up. "I've got to write up my video idea."

I finished my strawberry yogurt. When I walked out of the dining hall I walked right into the middle of an argument – between Natalie and Dana! Kristen Lindquist and Brooke Miller were standing off to the side. They didn't look very happy.

"No fair, Natalie," Dana said. Her face was red.

"It's totally fair, Dana," Natalie shot back. She turned to me. "What do you think, Mary-Kate?"

"About what?" I asked, stepping between them. That, Diary, was my first mistake.

Dana put her hands on her hips. "Kristen and Brooke are my best friends," she declared.

I glanced at Kristen and Brooke. Kristen stared at her shoes. Brooke bit her lip.

"Okay," I agreed. "And this is a problem because . . . "

"Because Kristen and Brooke already signed *my* nomination form," Natalie said.

"We didn't know Dana was going to run for Prom Princess, Mary-Kate," Brooke explained.

"I decided at the last minute," Dana huffed.

Kristen looked up from her shoes. "If we had known you were going to run, Dana, we wouldn't have signed Natalie's form. Honest."

I could tell Kristen and Brooke were upset. Dana is the leader of White Oak's snobby crowd. Signing Natalie's form instead of Dana's for Prom Princess was a really bad move for Brooke and Kristen.

"Cross Kristen's and Brooke's names off your form right now, Natalie," Dana demanded. Her voice got louder. "So they can sign mine."

"Once you've signed someone's form, you can't change your mind and sign someone else's form instead," Natalie insisted. Her voice got louder, too.

20

I did *not* want to be in the middle of Dana and Natalie's problem. I had no idea how to solve it! I was glad when Mrs. Weinstock, the dining hall supervisor, interrupted.

"What's going on here?" Mrs. Weinstock asked.

Natalie, Dana, Kristen, Brooke and I all began talking at once.

"Natalie's being a jerk," Dana snapped.

"I am not!" Natalie's temper flared. "You are!"

"It's all our fault," Brooke said.

"But we didn't know," Kristen added.

"It's just a misunderstanding," I said.

"Enough!" Mrs. Weinstock held up her hands. "Since you girls can't settle your differences peacefully, we'll let Mrs. Pritchard do it."

Great, I thought as Mrs. Weinstock pointed towards the Administration Building. Ashley has told me a thousand times to mind my own business, Diary. Next time I'll listen.

The five of us formed a line in front of Mrs. Pritchard's desk. The headmistress smoothed her short silver hair. Her rhinestone glasses were hanging on a chain around her neck. "What seems to be the problem?" she asked.

"Natalie won't let Brooke and Kristen sign my Prom Princess nomination form," Dana said.

"Because they already signed mine!" Natalie cried.

"Only because we didn't know Dana was running," Brooke protested.

"That's right," Kristen said.

"Why are you here, Mary-Kate?" Mrs. Pritchard asked.

"Natalie, uh, asked my opinion," I explained. "But I don't really have one."

"I see." Mrs. Pritchard sat back and folded her hands.

Everyone waited. That was a *long* minute.

"I'm sorry, Dana, but I have to agree with Natalie about this," Mrs. Pritchard said. "No crossing out of names after signing. That would be too confusing."

"But Kristen and Brooke are my friends," Dana said.

"I understand, Dana," Mrs. Pritchard said. "But if I let them change their votes, then I have to let other girls change their votes, too. If too many people start switching at the last minute, it will be a mess. We might even have girls signing more than one form."

Mrs. Pritchard stood and showed us out of her door. "Goodbye, girls," she said. Then she turned her attention to another girl waiting to see her.

As soon as we got into the hall, Natalie shot Dana a smug look and hurried away.

"We're sorry, Dana," Kristen murmured.

"We really do want to sign your form," Brooke added.

"Forget it," Dana snapped. "This is all Mary-Kate's fault."

"Why is it my fault?" I asked. Somehow Dana always makes me the bad guy. It's amazing.

"You could have just told Natalie to let me have Kristen's and Brooke's signatures, Mary-Kate, but *nooooo*." Dana rolled her eyes.

"Do you really think Natalie would have agreed just because I said so, Dana?" I asked.

Dana was too angry to listen. "I won't forget this, Mary-Kate."

I hate to say this, Diary, because I know it's not nice, but I sure hope Dana doesn't become our school Prom Princess!

Dear Diary,

I've got the green light for the Prom Princess video! That's what they say in Hollywood when a project is approved. And Mr. Shanks made a suggestion to make the video even better.

"Make one of the contestants the 'star' of your video," he said. "Audiences care more about someone they can get to know."

That's a great idea, I thought. *But which contestant?*

Mr. Shanks handed out the digital video cameras we were going to use and explained how they worked. After the meeting Phoebe and I raced back to our room. Phoebe sat cross-legged on her bed and read the whole instruction book cover to cover.

I labelled a spiral notebook with the name of our project. I wanted to keep a record of every shot.

"Okay, Madame Director, what do we do first?" Phoebe asked.

I picked up the notebook and a pen. "We find our star!"

Since it was dinnertime, Phoebe and I headed straight for the dining hall. Phoebe was going to videotape my interviews with all the Prom Princess contestants. We could decide later which shots to use, once we decided who the star of our video was going to be.

I spotted Marsha Avery sitting on a bench outside the dining hall.

"Hey, Ashley!" Marsha said, holding out a clipboard and a pen. "Do you want to sign my Prom Princess form?"

"Not right now," I said. I planned to sign for the girl who starred in my video. So did Mary-Kate, Campbell and Phoebe. "I'm making a video about the Prom Princess contest—"

"You are?" Marsha interrupted, frowning at the camera. "Now?"

Marsha looked upset. Maybe she was worried about her hair or her outfit. I tried to make her calm. "These shots don't have to be in it," I said.

"I don't want to be in it at all!" Marsha exclaimed.

"You don't?" I was surprised. I thought having a video crew follow you everywhere would be fun.

Marsha stared down at her clipboard. "I only have eight signatures," she whispered. "If I lose, I don't want to be totally embarrassed in a video."

I could see her point. "I understand," I said. I spotted Lavender Duncan going into the dining hall. "Catch you later," I told Marsha.

Phoebe and I followed Lavender across the dining room. We waited until she went through the dinner line and sat at a table near the window. She was fluffing her short brown hair as I stopped at her table.

"Hey, Lavender," I said, "can I sit down?"

"Sure!" Lavender smiled brightly, and her grey eyes sparkled. "What's up?"

I saw the nomination form clipped to Lavender's notebook. Most of the lines on Lavender's form were filled in. She was doing much better than Marsha.

"I'm making a movie about the Prom Princess contest," I said. "Do you want to be in it?"

"Me?" Lavender looked confused. "Why me?"

"Uh . . ." I didn't have a good answer. Phoebe and I had just asked the first two contestants we saw. I pointed to Lavender's binder. "Your nomination form is almost full," I said.

"True," Lavender said. "All my friends signed for me this morning. But I don't think it will be enough to make me a finalist."

"You still have time to ask for more signatures, don't you?" I asked.

Lavender shrugged. "I don't think I can ask girls I don't know! I get tongue-tied when I have to answer questions out loud in class." She looked past me and gasped. "Is that camera on?" she asked, pointing at Phoebe.

"Yes, it is," I said. I suddenly had a good interview idea. I waved for Phoebe to move closer. "Can you tell me why you want to be the Prom Princess, Lavender?"

"You want me to talk? To the camera?" Lavender's grey eyes widened. Her mouth dropped open a little.

"Lavender?" I leaned closer. "Are you okay?"

Lavender didn't answer. She just stared at the camera.

"I'm turning it off," Phoebe said. She pressed the pause button and lowered the camera.

Lavender let out a long, slow breath. Then she smiled at me. "Sorry, Ashley. I'm just not good at this sort of thing."

"That's okay," I said. "Good luck with the contest."

"Now what?" Phoebe asked as we walked towards an empty table.

"Let's hope we have better luck with Natalie," I said. "Because I do *not* want Dana to be our star!"

Phoebe and I caught up with Natalie after dinner in the Student Union. She was playing a video game. After she scored, I quickly explained my video project.

"You want to videotape *everything* I do?" Natalie asked.

"Yes," I said. "I'm going to tape the whole contest from start to finish."

"That sounds like fun," she said. "But if I say yes, I have a few rules. No taping while I'm eating." She wrinkled her nose. "Nobody looks good when they're chewing."

27

Natalie had a point, but I suddenly had a bad feeling about her being my star.

"No taping without telling me," Natalie went on. "And I get to choose which shots of me you can use."

I could tell it would be tricky to work with her.

"We'll let you know if we decide to cast you, Natalie," Phoebe said. She shut off the camera and slapped the screen closed. "Right, Ashley?" She shot me a look that said *"No way!"*

"Right," I said. I grabbed Phoebe's arm and hurried her away. I knew Natalie wouldn't be our star. But now we didn't *have* a star!

Phoebe and I sat on a bench outside our dorm, Porter House. "There's only one person left," Phoebe said.

I shook my head. "I absolutely will *not* ask Dana to star in our video."

"Okay – but who then?" Phoebe asked. She shrugged. "Maybe Marsha will change her mind."

"Maybe," I said. "But eight nominations aren't enough to make her a finalist."

"I'll sign for you, Ashley," Amber Fleming said, passing by. She stopped in front of me and pulled a pen out of her bag. "Do you have your form with you?"

"My form?" I said, confused.

"For the Prom Princess contest," Amber said. "I think it would be awesome if you won."

"Oh, no." I shook my head. "I'm not running for Prom Princess. I'm just making a video about it."

Phoebe looked up sharply.

"Well, let me know if you change your mind," Amber said and waved as she walked away.

Phoebe was staring at me.

"What?" I said.

"You should star in the video, Ashley," Phoebe said. She picked up the camera and pointed it straight at me.

"Me?" My mouth dropped open.

"All our friends would nominate you in a second," Phoebe said. "Lots of other girls would, too. You're the only hope for our video."

"I don't know . . ." I said.

"Remember," Phoebe added, "it's you or Dana."

That decided it. "Me," I declared.

And that, Diary, means I have to run for Prom Princess!

Chapter 3

Friday

Dear Diary,

Now that I'm running for Prom Princess, I realise how cool it would be to win!

There's more to being Prom Princess than just the tiara. First of all, it's a big honour. It means girls in all the grades think you are the ideal White Oak student: well-rounded, smart, kind, loyal and fun!

 And, Diary, once a Prom Princess, always a Prom Princess. The former Prom Princesses have a welcoming party for the new one. There's even a newsletter sent around by grown-up Prom Princesses.

Just imagine, Diary, when I'm ninety-nine years old I could be telling some future First Form girl what it was like to be a Prom Princess.

If I win, of course!

"You're up early." Phoebe sat up and stretched.

"Excited, I guess," I said. I put aside my diary and picked up the spiral notebook. "And nervous.

We're going to need a really great video if we want ours to be chosen for the film festival!"

Phoebe nodded and ran her hands through her curly brown hair. "The other girls came up with some awesome ideas."

It's true, Diary. Jessie Lang and Alyssa Fuji are videotaping a department store's makeover of a girl, and then seeing if people treat the girl differently after her makeover. Abigail Fitch's video is about roommates. Taylor Cranston and Ellen Withers are going to show what it's like to be a teacher at White Oak. Blair Clark's video is called *The Life and Death of a Green Bean*. Now that's not too exciting – is it, Diary?

"I have an idea how to start," I told Phoebe.

"Let's hear it," Phoebe said.

I swivelled my chair to face her. "Our first scene should be about the contest. We can use shots of the other girls getting signatures, with my voice explaining the rules. We'll end that part when I decide to run."

"I love it!" Phoebe beamed. "We have all the contestants on camera except for Dana. I'll film her today."

"Next we'll tape me collecting signatures," I said.

"We need to get some signatures at breakfast," Phoebe said, jumping out of bed. "Everyone else has a major head start. Even Dana!"

I had been so busy planning the video, I hadn't thought about how much work we had to do for the contest. Our video would be a total flop if I didn't make it as a finalist!

We got showered and dressed. Just before leaving for breakfast, I put the Prom Princess form on a clipboard.

"Wait!" Phoebe said. She turned the camera on and handed it to me.

"What are you doing?" I asked as she picked up a pen.

"Film this," she said. She made a big show of signing her name on the top line. "Your first nomination," she said.

"Now it's official!" I said, giggling.

We left the room and ran into Tammi Patterson coming down the hall. Phoebe stood back with the camera running.

"Hi, Tammi!" I said. "I just decided to run for Prom Princess. Will you sign my form?"

"You'd be perfect, Ashley," Tammi said. "But I signed Dana's form last night."

"Oh," I said. I tried not to look disappointed. Phoebe was still taping. And I didn't want Tammi to feel bad.

"I'm really sorry, Ashley," Tammi said. Then she pointed toward the stairs. Layne Wagner and Carmen Barnes were just starting down. "Maybe they'll sign for you."

"Thanks." I hurried over to Layne and Carmen. Phoebe jogged after me with the camera. On the second floor we caught up with the two girls. "Hi, guys!"

"Hey, Ashley!" Carmen smiled. "What's up?"

"I decided to run for Prom Princess," I said. "Will you sign my form?"

"I can't," Layne said. "I already voted for Lavender."

"Me too," Carmen said.

"I understand," I said. Both girls were good friends with Lavender. I forced a smile. "See you later."

Phoebe and I waited until Layne and Carmen had gone.

"Don't worry, Ashley," Phoebe said. "I know for a fact that Summer and Elise haven't signed for anyone yet."

I was glad to hear that, but Summer Sorenson and Elise Van Hook were only two people. I needed more signatures than that!

That's why I'm worried, Diary. What if everyone

I know has already nominated someone else? Is it too late?

Dear Diary,
  "Wow! Ashley has fifty signatures!" I exclaimed.

  "Awesome," Campbell said.

  We were sitting on the bleachers by the dugout. The rest of the team was hanging out, waiting for Coach Hadley. She was announcing our positions today.

  I promised Ashley I would ask the girls on the softball team to sign her form. Summer and Elise were collecting signatures for her at the library while Ashley went to her Young Filmmakers Club meeting.

  "That's amazing." Campbell was impressed. "She started two days late!"

  My sister might actually win, I realised. I hoped so. Now that Ashley had entered the contest, she really wanted to be Prom Princess.

  "I'll sign it." Campbell took my pen and signed the form.

  "I want to nominate Ashley, too," our teammate, Sonya Perez, said. She took the pen and clipboard from Campbell.

"Wait a minute!" Dana said, walking out of the dugout. "Sonya, you said you'd sign for me!"

I groaned inside. I had forgotten that Dana would be at the field to hear Coach Hadley's announcement for her newspaper article.

"Well, I said that before I knew Ashley was running," Sonya said.

"That's just great!" Dana glared at me, then stalked back into the dugout.

"Is she still mad at you?" Campbell asked.

"Dana is *always* mad at me," I said. "Or maybe she's upset because she isn't getting as many signatures as she expected."

I collected several other signatures. Dana sat in the dugout, watching everything with a frown.

Natalie came up from behind me. "Ashley is doing pretty great, huh?" she said, looking over my shoulder.

"So far," I said. I glanced at the clipboard and realised that the top sheet was completely filled!

"I want you to know I'm not upset that most of the softball team signed for Ashley," Natalie said. "I already have more than enough signatures to be a finalist."

"That's great," I said. I wondered how she could know that she had enough names. Had she counted everyone's signatures?

"Okay, girls!" Coach Hadley called from the field.

I pressed the metal clip on the board and slid a blank nomination form on top.

Natalie dropped her clipboard. Her pages fell out when the clipboard hit the ground. "Oops!" She stooped to pick up the loose papers.

"Come on, Mary-Kate!" Campbell waved me onto the field. "Coach is going to announce our positions!"

I left Ashley's clipboard on the seat and dashed to join my teammates. I hoped Coach Hadley would assign me to first base!

Natalie ran to the dugout and put her clipboard away. Then she joined the rest of us on the field.

"White Oak is going to have a great team this year," Coach Hadley began. "Everyone played so well at tryouts it was hard to decide which positions you should play."

I heard footsteps on the bleachers. Dana had left the dugout and was now sitting on the bleachers. But she wasn't taking notes for the newspaper. She was flipping through the nomination forms on Ashley's clipboard.

I felt my face grow hot. I couldn't say or do *anything* – not during practice.

Coach assigned us to our positions – and I got my wish: first base! Then we started the game. I was up at bat first. I glanced back at the bleachers again.

Great. Now Dana was staring straight at me. She had her notebook on her lap and her pen in her hand.

This one is for you, Dana. I gripped the bat. *I'm going to hit this over the fence.*

I swung – and gasped! Pain shot through my arm, and I dropped the bat. I bit my lip trying to fight back tears. My arm *burned!*

Oh, no! I thought as Coach ran over. *Will I still be able to play softball?*

Chapter 4

Saturday

Dear Diary,

Summer and Elise saved seats in the dining hall for me and Phoebe. We got there a little late because of our Young Filmmakers Club meeting. Mr. Shanks gave us more pointers, and everyone talked about how they were making their videos. It was fun – and inspiring!

And I even got three more signatures from girls in the club!

"Elise and I got ten signatures at the library for you," Summer said. She took a bite of her veggie lasagna.

"Really?" I was impressed. "That's great."

"How many signatures do you have now, Ashley?" Elise asked.

"I'm not sure," I said. "That depends on how many Mary-Kate got at softball practice." I glanced around the dining hall, but I didn't see Mary-Kate anywhere. "Where is she?"

"I don't know," Phoebe said. Then she pointed at the door. "But here comes Campbell."

"Where's Mary-Kate?" I asked when Campbell sat down.

"Mary-Kate hurt her arm at softball practice," Campbell explained. "The nurse sent her back to our room."

"Is she okay?" I stood up and started gathering my stuff. I had to go check on my sister!

"You can sit down, Ashley," Campbell said. "She's fine. She just has to rest her arm."

"Will Mary-Kate be able to play in the first game next week?" Summer asked.

"The nurse just said Mary-Kate can't practise for a few days," Campbell explained.

I groaned. "Mary-Kate is *not* going to like that!" My sister was really psyched about trying to beat that home-run record. Being benched was not going to make her very happy!

After dinner, Campbell, Phoebe and I went to check on Mary-Kate. She was sitting on her bed holding an ice pack on her upper arm. She looked really glad to see us. "Hey, guys!"

"How are you doing?" I asked. "Campbell told us you got hurt at practice."

"Not great," Mary-Kate admitted. "The nurse said I pulled a muscle. But" – she grinned – "I got lots of signatures for you!"

"Super!" I smiled. I handed Mary-Kate a bowl of macaroni I brought for her from the dining hall.

"Should we film me counting the nominations?" I asked Phoebe.

"Good idea!" she said and reached for the camera.

I unfolded the form I used at the Young Filmmakers Club meeting and the one I had given Summer to use at the library. "I have to add these to the whole collection," I said.

"Your clipboard is on my desk," Mary-Kate said.

"So how many do you have total, Ashley?" Phoebe asked from behind the camera.

"Sixty-three plus the ten softball players equals seventy-three!" I grinned. "Is that enough to make me a finalist?"

"I hope so," Mary-Kate said.

"Me too," Campbell added.

"Hold up all the sheets so I can videotape them," Phoebe suggested.

"Okay." I pressed the metal clip on the clipboard and removed the pages. There were two blank forms under the page Mary-Kate had filled up. But the two pages *I* had filled up weren't there. "Mary-Kate, where are my other two pages I filled up?"

"What do you mean?" Mary-Kate asked. "Aren't they on the clipboard?"

I looked again. And then again. But no matter how many times I flipped through the pages, it came out the same each time.

My votes weren't there.

Dear Diary,

What happened to Ashley's signatures?

"The sheets have to be here somewhere," I said. I started to panic. As soon as I moved, though, a pain in my arm made me yelp!

"You stay still," Campbell ordered me. "We'll look."

Ashley, Campbell and Phoebe searched the room. Phoebe looked in the wastebasket and under my bed. Ashley went through all of my desk drawers. Campbell checked the wardrobe and the dressing table. They searched anyplace a piece of paper could be hiding.

Ashley looked really upset, and I didn't blame her. I was upset, too – since *I* was the one who lost her signatures: forty of them!

"Those pages didn't just disappear," Phoebe said.

"Think back, Mary-Kate," Ashley said. "When was the last time you saw them?"

I bit my lip, trying to remember. "The pages were on the clipboard when Campbell signed," I said. "I had just counted them. Then Lexy Martin and eight other softball players signed."

"And that filled up the third form," Campbell added.

"So I pulled out a new form," I said. "Maybe that's when the pages dropped out! They're probably under the bleachers."

"Let's go look," Ashley said.

I wasn't going to stay in my room while they searched. I carefully put on my jacket, and then Campbell, Phoebe, 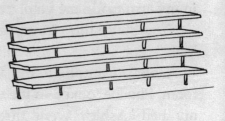 Ashley and I hurried to the softball field. It was starting to get dark, but we searched everywhere.

We didn't find Ashley's nomination forms.

"Do you have enough signatures to be a Prom Princess finalist without the missing sheets?" Campbell asked.

Ashley shook her head. "I don't think so. I'll only have thirty-three votes."

Phoebe looked through a trash container by the bleachers. "No nomination forms in here."

"Well, I'm not going to give up," I said. "Maybe someone on the softball team saw what happened to them."

Campbell looked at her watch. "It's almost curfew. We'd better hurry if we want to ask them tonight."

Ashley and Phoebe left to search the path from the field to Porter House. Campbell and I ran to Phipps House, another dorm.

Not a single girl we asked from the softball team knew anything about the missing forms.

"That's everyone in this house," I said.

"Except Dana," Campbell said. "She was at the field working on her article for the *Acorn*."

I gasped. "I saw Dana looking through Ashley's clipboard when Coach Hadley announced the positions."

"Do you think Dana *took* Ashley's forms?" Campbell asked.

"I don't know," I said. "She didn't look too happy when she flipped through Ashley's pages."

Diary, did Dana want to be Prom Princess so badly, she'd steal someone else's nomination forms?

Chapter 5

Sunday

Dear Diary,

I wish I had better news to report, but I don't. Phoebe and I looked everywhere between the softball field and Porter House last night. We couldn't find my missing forms. No one Mary-Kate asked has seen them, either.

Right before curfew Phoebe and I found three girls who had signed the missing forms. When I told them what had happened, they signed my new form. But that's only three out of forty!

Today Phoebe and I tried to find more girls who had signed my lost pages. The deadline was noon! My chance of being a finalist was slipping away.

"Are you sure you want me to keep taping?" Phoebe asked.

I nodded. "We need a movie for the Young Filmmakers Club, even if it's about *losing* the Prom Princess contest."

Susanna Worley came out of the Student Union. "Susanna!" I called.

Susanna was happy to nominate me again. We ran into two other girls heading for the Harrington School for Boys' lacrosse team practice on our school's field. They signed for me a second time, too.

Prom Princess

"Maybe there will be some more girls at practice," I said. We headed for the playing field.

"Hey, there's Ross!" Phoebe exclaimed.

Ross Lambert is my boyfriend. He's really smart and totally cute. I hadn't seen Ross much the past week because the Harrington lacrosse team had been practising every day for the county finals.

"Hi, Ashley!" Ross ran to the edge of the field. He pointed to my clipboard. "Are you still collecting signatures?"

"I've got half an hour before I have to hand them in," I said.

"Move closer together, you two!" Phoebe waved her hand and aimed the camera.

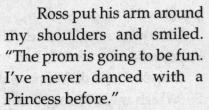

Ross put his arm around my shoulders and smiled. "The prom is going to be fun. I've never danced with a Princess before."

"I have to win the contest first," I reminded him.

"How can you miss, Ashley?" Ross said. He gave me a sly grin. "Especially when you've got *me* as your Prince?" He winked at the camera.

45

I gave him a playful punch on the arm. Then the coach called him back onto the lacrosse field.

"That will be one of the best scenes in the whole movie!" Phoebe declared. She checked her watch. "We'd better go hand in your forms."

Phoebe and I arrived at the Administration Building at eleven-fifty exactly. Phoebe kept filming.

Dana rushed toward us.

"Smile, Dana!" Phoebe said. "You're on camera!"

Dana just scowled.

"How many signatures did you get?" I asked.

"That's my business, not yours." Dana clutched her forms to her chest and hurried through the door.

Phoebe lowered the camera. "What's her problem?"

"I don't know," I said. Then it hit me. The one explanation for Dana's bad mood.

Maybe Dana didn't have very many signatures.

Which meant I might still have a chance to be a Prom Princess finalist!

Dear Diary,

I asked myself questions all night! Did I drop Ashley's forms? I don't know. Did Dana find them? I don't know. Did she take the sheets off the clipboard? I don't know.

Still, I had a funny feeling that Dana had my sister's nomination forms. But I couldn't prove it.

At dinner tonight Ashley told Summer and Elise about the missing forms.

"What rotten luck, Ashley," Elise said. "You worked so hard to get all those signatures."

"You don't know what happened to them?" Summer asked.

"They probably fell off my clipboard," Ashley said. "I can't do anything about it now."

I smiled at my sister. She hadn't told anyone that it was my fault her pages were lost.

Dana, Kristen, Brooke and Lisa Dunmead stopped at the table next to us. "Let's sit over here," Dana declared. She walked around to the far side of the table. Kristen, Brooke and Lisa followed her. "I don't want Mary-Kate's losing streak to rub off on me."

"What losing streak?" Kristen asked.

"You know how Mary-Kate wants to break the home-run record?" Dana said. "Well, she can't bat now that she hurt her arm!"

My cheeks burned, but I kept quiet. Dana was right – which made me feel even worse.

"Losing runs in Mary-Kate's family this week," Dana went on.

"It does?" Lisa said.

Dana nodded. "I don't think Ashley has much chance of being a Prom Princess finalist."

Ashley's head snapped up.

No one knew what to say – except me. I turned to face Dana. "What makes you so sure Ashley doesn't have a chance?" I asked.

"Oh, come on now. Ashley started *two* days late," Dana said. She rolled her eyes with a smug smile.

I couldn't let Dana get away with insulting Ashley!

I was so angry, Diary, that before I could think about what I was saying, I blurted out, "I know what you did, Dana. I know you stole Ashley's nomination forms!"

Chapter 6

Sunday

Dear Diary,

I couldn't believe my ears. Mary-Kate accused Dana Woletsky of *stealing* my nomination forms!

Everyone at our table was stunned. The whole dining hall got quiet.

"Are you calling me a thief, Mary-Kate?" Dana said, looking shocked.

"If the name fits, Dana," Mary-Kate shot back.

"You know," Campbell said, "I saw Dana looking at the clipboard Mary-Kate left on the bleachers yesterday."

Phoebe gasped. "Is that why you wouldn't show Ashley your nomination forms at the Administration Building today, Dana?" She kept the camera rolling. "Because you knew Ashley would recognise the names of girls who voted for *her*?"

"No!" Dana shook her head. "I didn't want to tell because I didn't want to jinx my chances."

"Do you expect us to believe that, Dana?" Campbell asked.

"I believe it," Brooke said.

"Me too," Kristen said. Lisa nodded.

"Well, I don't," Cheryl Miller said from another table. "Dana was mad because I signed Ashley's form instead of hers."

Summer glared at Dana. "Taking someone else's forms is really low, Dana."

"I didn't do anything," Dana insisted. "And you can't prove that I did."

I looked around the dining hall. It was obvious from all the whispering and pointing that Dana's closest friends were the only ones who believed her story.

That won't help me, though, Diary. The nomination forms have already been turned in. And Dana will get credit for my signatures!

Dear Diary,

Coach Hadley called me into her office right before my P.E. class was about to begin.

"I spoke to the nurse, Mary-Kate," Coach said. "She doesn't want you to play any sports until our first game on Friday."

"Why not?" I asked.

"So your arm can heal," the coach explained.

"My arm feels fine." I swung my arm around to prove it. It was a little stiff, but it didn't hurt. "I'll lose my batting edge if I don't practise for four days!"

"It won't take you long to get your edge back," Coach Hadley said.

"But I have to bat my *best* on Friday," I explained. "I'm trying to break the home-run record. I can't do that if I don't practise."

"You won't break *any* records if your injury gets worse, Mary-Kate," the coach pointed out.

We were interrupted by a knock on the door. Dana stuck her head inside. "Excuse me, Coach Hadley," she said. "I came to pick up the Mighty Oaks' game schedule for the *Acorn*."

"I'll be with you in a moment, Dana," Coach Hadley said.

"Okay," Dana said and stepped back into the hall.

Coach looked back at me. "You are not to practise softball until the nurse checks your arm on Friday morning, Mary-Kate – or I'll have to bench you for the game, too."

"Okay, Coach," I said. I could tell it wouldn't do any good to argue.

"You can do homework in the library during P.E. today," Coach Hadley said.

Dana glared at me as I left. I ignored her. I didn't care if she was mad at me for telling everyone she had taken Ashley's signatures.

I headed towards the library with my glove, ball and books.

My arm felt stiff. I bent and straightened it a few times. That seemed to help a bit. *I don't have to bat to keep my arm in shape,* I realised. *I just have to work the muscles.*

And I can do that right here! I stopped at the back door of the library. I set down my books and slipped on my glove.

I threw the ball at the brick building and caught it when it bounced back. My arm felt tight, but after a while it started to loosen up.

"What are you doing, Mary-Kate?" Dana asked

 from behind me. Her voice took me by surprise.

"Going to the library," I said, turning to face Dana. I hid my glove behind my back.

The softball bounced off the building and hit the ground. It rolled past me toward Dana.

"No, you're not, Mary-Kate. You're practising!"

Dana exclaimed as she picked up the ball. "I just heard Coach Hadley tell you *not* to practise!"

I couldn't believe that *Dana* had caught me!

"Where are you going?" I asked when she turned and started walking away with my ball.

"To tell Coach Hadley you were practising!" she yelled back over her shoulder.

Oh, no! Will Coach Hadley really bench me so I can't play in Friday's game? If she does, I fumed, *it will be because of Dana!*

Dear Diary,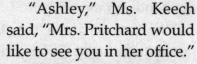

I was drawing a still life of fruit when Layne Wagner came into my art class today. She handed the teacher a note.

"Ashley," Ms. Keech said, "Mrs. Pritchard would like to see you in her office."

"Me?" I squeaked. Getting called out of class to see the headmistress is serious stuff! Everyone in the class stopped working to stare at me.

I took off my smock and hung it up. Then I grabbed my books.

"Ashley never gets in trouble!" Wendy whispered to Jolene as I walked by.

"I wonder what she did," Jolene whispered back.

Me too! I thought as I left.

My stomach was in knots when I got to the office. I couldn't figure out what I had done wrong.

The secretary pointed towards Mrs. Pritchard's door. "Go on in, Ashley."

My hand shook on the doorknob when I opened the door. I was surprised to see Natalie Pittman sitting across from Mrs. Pritchard's desk.

Are we both in trouble? I wondered as I walked inside. My head was spinning. I hate not knowing what's going on.

"Have a seat, Ashley," Mrs. Pritchard said.

I sat down with my books in my lap and folded my hands on top of them.

"We have a problem with your Prom Princess nomination forms," Mrs. Pritchard said. "I want to explain it so that there's no misunderstanding."

"What kind of problem?" I asked.

"The same eight girls signed nomination forms for both of you," Mrs. Pritchard explained.

"Eight?" I repeated the word. My mind did some quick maths. Eight girls had signed for me a second time between Saturday night and Sunday noon.

"A student cannot nominate two people. That's the rule," the headmistress said. "We'll be subtracting those eight names from each of your totals."

"That seems fair," Natalie said.

I just stared. A terrible truth suddenly became clear: the only way there could be any duplication would be if Natalie had taken my forms.

Natalie cheated.

And Dana hadn't!

What should I do? I wondered. *This isn't fair at all!*

Natalie wouldn't lose much if eight nominations were taken away from her total. She had my *other* thirty-two signers!

I had to tell the truth.

"Hmmm . . . well—" I tried to begin, but Mrs. Pritchard wasn't finished.

"I don't think anyone meant to break the rules," Mrs. Pritchard continued. "I'm sure the girls who signed twice just didn't want to say 'No' to a friend."

"Probably not," Natalie said, smiling at the headmistress. She didn't look at me.

"Actually, that's not—" I started. Then I stopped.

At school, being a tattletale was almost as bad as being a thief. I couldn't rat out Natalie.

"It's a good thing nobody cheated," Mrs. Pritchard said. "I'd have to cancel the Prom Princess contest. That's never happened before."

That made me glad I hadn't said anything. I didn't want to be responsible for ending the Prom Princess contest – not after it has been a tradition for over one hundred years!

"Are we good here, girls?" Mrs. Pritchard stood and opened her door for us.

"I'm okay with it," Natalie said, standing up. "How about you, Ashley?" She looked straight at me.

"I'm fine, too," I said, meeting her stare. "Just fine."

"Excellent. I'm glad we're done with that problem," Mrs. Pritchard said as she left the office. Natalie and I followed her out.

This isn't done, Natalie, I thought. *Not between us this isn't. There is no way I'm letting you be Prom Princess.*

Chapter 7

Monday

Dear Diary,

I was so angry with Natalie, I couldn't get anything done. In class I kept daydreaming that Natalie won the Prom Princess contest and I ran up onto the stage and snatched the glittering tiara off her head!

And worst of all, I couldn't talk to anyone about it! Mary-Kate had softball practice, and Phoebe had a dentist appointment. I had to wait until I saw them at dinner.

But at dinner Cheryl, Lexy, Summer and Elise sat down with us, too. I wanted to tell Mary-Kate and Phoebe what had happened, but there were too many people around.

Besides, Mary-Kate had a problem, too.

"Coach Hadley benched you?" Campbell asked.

Mary-Kate nodded. "The nurse said I couldn't practise until Friday. I was just throwing a ball, trying to keep my arm limber, but Dana saw me and told Coach Hadley."

"Dana should know that the Mighty Oaks have a better chance of winning if *you* play, Mary-Kate," Lexy said.

"I guess Dana doesn't care about the team," Phoebe said.

Campbell nodded. "Maybe Dana just wanted to get even with Mary-Kate for telling everyone that she took Ashley's forms."

Inside, I felt sick. Everyone still thought Dana had taken my nomination forms. I glanced towards Dana's table.

Dana was sitting with Brooke and Kristen. Everyone else was giving Dana the silent treatment.

If I blabbed about Natalie, though, everyone would start talking about it. The headmistress would find out and cancel the Prom Princess contest. Then it would be *my* fault that the tradition would end – possibly forever.

"There's Mrs. Pritchard. She's going to announce the finalists!" Summer exclaimed.

Phoebe had turned off the camera so she could eat. She picked it up again when Mrs. Pritchard entered. She hit the record button.

Mrs. Pritchard raised her hand for quiet.

All of my friends crossed their fingers for luck –

except Phoebe, of course, who needed her fingers to run the camera.

"It's time to announce our two finalists for Prom Princess," Mrs. Pritchard said. "First, with the most nominations is . . . "

Mary-Kate squeezed my arm.

"Natalie Pittman!" Mrs. Pritchard said, applauding.

"Oh!" Natalie looked surprised. "I can't believe it!"

What a fake! She's not surprised at all, I thought. But I smiled. I was *not* going to be a poor sport.

"Way to go, Natalie!" Rachel stood up and whistled.

"Yea, Natalie!" Tammi yelled.

A bunch of girls cheered. Natalie had got a lot of support *without* my signatures. Natalie waved and smiled. *How could Natalie be happy when she cheated to win?* I wondered.

I wanted to win, too. But my being honest was more important.

Mrs. Pritchard waved for quiet. "The second finalist is . . ."

"Please let it be Ashley," Mary-Kate murmured next to me.

"Dana Woletsky!" Mrs. Pritchard applauded again.

"Me?" Dana jumped out of her seat. "This is so cool!"

There was an awkward moment of silence.

"White Oak students are *always* good sports," Mrs. Pritchard said, frowning.

A few girls took the hint and applauded. But no one said a word until the headmistress left.

Then a lot of girls in the dining hall began to whisper and point at Dana. They were upset because they thought Dana had cheated. Nobody wanted her to be a finalist.

Diary, I knew who the cheater was, and it wasn't Dana. I had to do something. But I didn't know what!

Dear Diary,

Dana looked shocked when Mrs. Pritchard called her name. I was shocked, too – I had no idea Dana was such a big faker!

"Dana looked like she didn't *expect* to be one of the finalists," I said to my sister.

"She probably didn't," Ashley whispered in my ear.

"Why not?" I whispered back. "Dana had her signatures and yours. Being a finalist was a sure thing for her."

"It wasn't Dana. I know for a fact that she didn't take my signatures, Mary-Kate," Ashley said.

"What?" I gasped. "I was totally wrong about her?"

"Totally," Ashley whispered. "I'll explain later in private."

Diary, I was stunned! I glanced at Dana again.

"Cheater," Carmen sneered. She was sitting behind Dana. The other girls at her table frowned. Even Brooke and Kristen looked embarrassed to be with Dana.

"But I—" Dana looked around the dining hall with a hurt expression.

Everyone thinks Dana took Ashley's nomination forms, I realised, *because of me.*

Dana has never apologised for the mean things she's done to me. But I had to do the right thing. I stood up. "Dana didn't do anything wrong," I said.

All eyes suddenly turned on me.

"What are you saying, Mary-Kate?" Cheryl asked.

I didn't know what proof Ashley had. But I needed some kind of explanation. "I didn't *see* Dana take Ashley's forms," I said. "The forms probably fell off the clipboard and blew away."

"I bet that's what happened," Ashley added.

Campbell and Phoebe exchanged a puzzled glance.

"I never should have accused you, Dana," I said.

"You're a finalist – fair and square." I started to applaud.

Ashley stood up and joined in. Then other girls in the dining hall started to applaud. Dana looked relieved.

Ashley leaned closer again. "Come to my room and bring Campbell. I'll tell you what's going on, but it's a secret."

"Okay," I agreed.

Campbell and I hurried to Ashley's room. We perched on the edge of Ashley's bed. Phoebe sat cross-legged on the floor. Ashley turned her desk chair to face us and sat down.

"Okay, Ashley," Phoebe said. "What's going on?"

"I got called to Mrs. Pritchard's office today." Ashley took a deep breath. "And so did Natalie."

"Why?" I asked.

"The same eight girls signed forms for both of us," Ashley said.

It took me a moment to understand what that meant.

"Eight!" Phoebe gasped. "That's how many girls signed for you a second time, Ashley. After your forms were lost."

My eyes got wide. "The same eight girls' names were on your form and Natalie's because *Natalie* was using your original forms!"

"Yep," Ashley said.

"Oh, no!" I slapped my hand to my forehead. "I remember now! Natalie was looking over my shoulder when I pulled a new form out of your clipboard."

"When the other forms fell out?" Ashley asked.

I nodded. "Natalie dropped her clipboard at the same time. Her papers fell off. I probably figured all the pages were hers."

"That was right when we were all called onto the field, wasn't it?" Campbell said.

I nodded. "So I was distracted. And Natalie must have picked up your forms when she picked up hers, Ashley."

"On purpose or by accident?" Phoebe asked.

"That doesn't matter now," I said. "Natalie *knew* she had Ashley's missing forms when she handed them in. All the contestants know exactly how many signatures they had *and* who signed their forms."

"So Dana is innocent," Campbell said. "And Natalie is a cheat."

"*And* a finalist," I pointed out.

"We can't let Natalie get away with this," Phoebe said. Her eyes flashed. "We've got to tell Mrs. Pritchard."

"We can't," Ashley said. "Nobody can tell *anyone*."

"Why not?" Campbell asked.

"If Mrs. Pritchard finds out that someone cheated," Ashley explained, "she'll cancel the Prom Princess contest. There might not be another one – ever."

"I don't want *that* to be our fault!" Campbell exclaimed.

"Neither do I," Phoebe said. "Besides, then Ashley and I won't have a movie project."

"But we can't let Natalie off the hook," I said.

"I agree, but we have to handle this ourselves," Ashley insisted. "No teachers or anything."

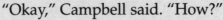

"Okay," Campbell said. "How?"

"I have an idea," Ashley said. "Natalie cheated to be the Prom Princess. So let's make sure she *doesn't* win."

"I love it!" Phoebe exclaimed.

"So do I," Campbell said. "It's the *perfect* payback."

"But how can we make sure Natalie doesn't get the most votes at the Spring Prom?" I asked.

"We'll make sure that *Dana* does," Ashley said.

My mouth fell open. "Are you crazy?"

Ashley shook her head. "It's the only way, Mary-Kate."

So that's where things stand, Diary. I'm going to help my worst enemy, Dana Woletsky, win the Prom Princess contest!

Chapter 8

Tuesday

Dear Diary,

Phoebe, Mary-Kate, Campbell and I stayed in my room until curfew. We came up with a plan to help Dana win the Prom Princess contest *and* save our video. Getting Dana to star in our video was only Phase One.

"What if Dana doesn't want to be in our video?" Phoebe asked the next morning.

"We can't take no for an answer," I said, "or we won't have a video at all."

"Right," Phoebe agreed, picking up the camera. "Do you think Dana can get more votes than Natalie at the dance?"

"Sure," I said. Getting more girls to vote for Dana was Phase Two. "Dana is one of the most popular girls in school."

"Even if she *is* bossy and a snob," Phoebe added with a grin. "At least she isn't a *cheat* like Natalie."

"Let's see what Summer and Elise found out," I said. My friends had agreed to ask other girls who they were going to vote for: Natalie or Dana.

Phoebe followed me out of our room and downstairs to the lounge. Summer and Elise were waiting for us on the sofa.

"Ashley, Phoebe," Elise said, waving us over.

"What did you guys find out?" I asked.

Phoebe stood back with the camera. I had told her to tape everything from now on. We didn't know which scenes would make our video more interesting.

"Half the girls we talked to are going to vote for Natalie," Elise said. "They think she's nicer than Dana and deserves it more."

I knew that wasn't true, but I couldn't say anything.

"Dana has the 'in crowd' vote tied up," Summer said.

I wasn't surprised to hear that. All the snobby girls stuck together.

"But the final Prom Princess vote will be by secret ballot," Elise added. "So things might change. If some girls don't have to worry that Dana will be mad at them, they might vote for Natalie instead of her."

The news wasn't great. It was going to be a very close race.

Phoebe put the camera on pause and followed me outside. "Kristen told me that Dana is at the *Acorn* working on her softball article."

"Let's go talk to her," I said as we headed across campus.

The *Acorn* office was crowded.
The next edition of the paper was
due out on Saturday.

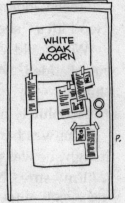

One girl was looking through a
stack of photos. Another girl was
typing at a computer. Ms. Bloomberg,
the faculty adviser for the newspaper,
was reading student articles. Taylor
and Ellen were filming the teacher for
their video project.

"There's Dana," I said, pointing. Dana was
sitting at a desk in the corner. We walked over.

"What do you want, Ashley?" Dana asked,
looking up. She frowned at Phoebe. "Turn the
camera off."

"I'm making a video about the Prom Princess
contest, Dana," I said. "You're a finalist, so I'd like
an interview."

"I'm too busy for your little video," Dana said.

I bit my lip. I wasn't sure if she was really busy
or still mad at Mary-Kate – and taking it out on me!

Phoebe looked at me. I could see she was trying
to figure out what to do. I got an idea. "Well, that's
too bad," I said. "I know, Phoebe, maybe Natalie
will do it. I'm sure that starring in a video might
help her get some extra Prom Princess votes."

Phoebe looked shocked. Then she caught on. "Good idea," she said.

"We should do everything we can to help her win," I added. "We don't want to make a video about a loser."

"Absolutely not," Phoebe agreed.

Dana was hanging on to every word now, even though she was pretending to ignore us.

"I'm sure Natalie will sign on," I said. "Especially when she finds out this video might be in the New Hampshire Film Festival."

Now Dana looked up. "Seriously?" she said. "A real film festival? With movie stars and everything?"

I smiled. "That's the one."

"All right," Dana agreed. "I'll do it."

I grinned. "Great!"

Phase One was now complete.

Dear Diary,

I went to softball practice today even though I couldn't play. I wanted to show my support for the team.

There was another reason I was there: I promised Ashley that I would help Dana win the Prom Princess contest. So I was going to try to convince my softball friends to vote for Dana instead of Natalie.

I know, Diary. I'm not thrilled about helping the one person at White Oak who seems to have it in for me. Life can really get strange.

Just as I expected, Dana was sitting in the bleachers taking notes for her article.

"Hi, Dana." I sat down beside her.

"What are you doing here?" Dana asked with a frown.

"I came to watch practice," I said, already annoyed. Then I reminded myself of Ashley's goal.

"I also wanted to apologise again," I said. I still felt bad for calling Dana a thief.

"Okay," Dana said. There was a long pause. Then she asked, "How's your arm?"

"Fine," I said, moving my arm around. "Not even a cramp."

"Good," Dana said. She turned to watch the field. I did, too.

Mindy was playing first base instead of me. That hurt, but I didn't let it show.

Brandy Oliver struck out. Campbell hit a pop fly into the outfield, but Caitlin missed it. Campbell was safe on first.

69

"You're supposed to catch it, Caitlin!" Dana shouted. "That should have been an easy out!"

I knew that Caitlin would probably vote for Dana. But that could change if Dana was mean to her. "Come on, Dana," I said. "This is just practice, not a game."

"Good thing," Dana said, rolling her eyes.

Natalie came up to bat next. She slammed a drive down the first base line, but Mindy wasn't paying attention. The ball whizzed right by her. Natalie ran to third, and Campbell crossed home plate.

"Wake up, Mindy!" Dana yelled. She shook her head and wrote something in her notebook.

"Are you writing about Caitlin's and Mindy's mistakes for your article, Dana?" I asked.

"A good reporter has to report the facts," Dana said. "It's not like I'm making it up."

"No, but the team practices so we don't make the same mistakes during a game," I explained. "Besides, I wouldn't want you to lose Caitlin's and Mindy's votes for Prom Princess."

"Since when do you care, Mary-Kate?" Dana snapped.

I couldn't tell Dana that Ashley and I wanted to help her win so that Natalie wouldn't. I shrugged.

"I just do, okay? So why not write good things about the team?"

"Because I want the Mighty Oaks to *win*," Dana said. "Mount Truman won the Conference Championship last year. They'll be a tough team to beat."

I was shocked. "If you're so worried about winning this Friday, why did you rat me out to Coach Hadley?" I asked.

"Because I want the Mighty Oaks to win the Conference Championship this year," Dana said. "That means *you* have to play the *other* eleven games this season."

"Huh?" I frowned, confused.

"You're one of the best hitters on the team, Mary-Kate," Dana said.

I was stunned to hear Dana admit that I was a good player.

"If you try to hit homers before your arm is okay," Dana went on, "you could be out for the whole season. Then White Oak might lose."

"But I might not be able to break Jamie Jerome's home-run record if I don't play on Friday," I blurted.

71

"What's more important to you, Mary-Kate – a championship for the whole team or a record for yourself?" Dana asked.

I didn't say anything, Diary, but I knew she was right: the team comes first.

I just didn't like hearing that from Dana!

Chapter 9

Thursday

Dear Diary,

Okay, Diary, tell me: why are people so difficult?

Dana wants my video to be the White Oak entry in the Film Festival so that she can be a star, right? So I thought she might be a little less snotty and a lot more cooperative than usual. That's a joke – on me! The problems started at breakfast.

Phoebe was taping Dana as she carried her tray to a table. As soon as she sat down, Dana made a chopping gesture with her hand. "Cut!" Dana ordered. "Turn the camera off!"

"What's the problem, Dana?" I asked.

"She's taping my left side," Dana said. "My *right* side is my best profile."

"Move to her right side, Phoebe," I said.

"Now *I* won't be in the picture," Brooke complained. She was sitting on Dana's right, behind Phoebe.

Kirsten, Brooke and Lisa all wanted to be in our video, now that Dana was the star.

"Pan the camera around the table so everyone gets in, Phoebe," I said. "Okay, everyone, just act natural."

Boy, was *that* a mistake, Diary! I shouldn't have said anything. Everyone started acting like robots!

"What – are – you – wearing – to – the – dance?" Kristen asked Dana. She paused between every word.

"A dress," Dana answered. She dipped her spoon into her oatmeal.

"Whatcolourisit?" Brooke asked. She ran all her words together.

"Gold," Dana said. "It totally rocks. Of course." She smirked. "Nobody here has the great taste that I do. I always dress better than everyone else."

"Cut!" I exclaimed. I couldn't use a scene with Dana insulting the clothing choices of the entire student body! "Phoebe and I have got to eat, too. See you later, Dana."

"But I haven't told you about my shoes," Dana protested.

"Later," Phoebe said, turning off the camera. "I'm starving." We went to sit with our friends at another table.

After breakfast, Phoebe and I followed Dana down the hall to our first class.

"What do you want me to do, Ashley?" Dana asked.

A documentary is a record of real people and events. I didn't want my video to look fake. "Just do what you usually do," I said.

We passed Holly Welsh and Jolene Dupree by the drinking fountain. They were talking about the Spring Prom.

"I'm wearing my hair up in these cute little glitter clips," Jolene was saying. "How are you wearing your hair?"

Holly shrugged. "The way I always do," she said. Her straight dark, hair was pulled back tightly and tied at the base of her neck.

Dana stopped. "You've *got* to do something different with your hair, Holly."

"B-but I always wear it like this," Holly said.

Dana raised an eyebrow. It was clear she didn't like Holly's hairstyle. "You should cut it short and curl it. That would soften your angular face."

"My what?" Holly looked upset. Something told me that she wasn't going to vote for Dana.

"No need to thank me." Dana smiled at her and moved on.

Phoebe skipped to get ahead of Dana. We wanted lots of different shots for the video.

"You know what, Phoebe? You should wear contacts," Dana said. "No one can see what colour your eyes are behind your glasses."

Phoebe frowned. I could tell she wasn't sure if Dana had just insulted her or not.

I flipped open my notebook and made a note: *Holly, hair; Phoebe, glasses: is Dana being mean, or is she trying to help?*

Later, at lunch, Phoebe, Dana and I sat with Layne and Carmen. They had nominated Lavender, but she wasn't a finalist. I hoped we could convince them to vote for Dana.

As usual, Phoebe had the camera ready and running when we started talking about the Spring Prom.

"Who are you going to the dance with, Dana?" Layne asked.

"Brent Lowell and Eric Mason both asked me," Dana said. "I decided to go with Brent."

"How could you decide?" Carmen asked. "They are both really cute guys."

"Brent's taller," Dana said. "I don't think the Prom Prince should be shorter than the Prom Princess, do you?"

"I guess not," Layne answered.

"She means *if* she wins the contest," I added.

Dana didn't seem to know that it was annoying when she sounded too confident.

"Who are you going to the dance with, Carmen?" Dana asked.

"I don't have a date," Carmen said.

"That's okay." Dana shrugged. "Nobody will say anything if you go to the Spring Prom alone – not to your face, anyway."

Carmen looked startled.

Dana really doesn't know that she just insulted Carmen, I realised. *That's probably another vote for Natalie.*

"I'm taking my camera to the prom," Phoebe said to break the tension. "But it's not a very good dancer."

Everyone laughed.

We had biology class after lunch. Blair was in the corner filming her green bean video.

"You're doing a movie about *this* bean plant, Blair?" Dana asked. She pointed to the potted plant on the windowsill. "It's wilted."

"No, it isn't," Blair said. She sounded annoyed. "I'm sure it's fine."

Actually, Dana was right. The bean plant looked limp.

"It's not fine," Dana said. "My grandmother's house is full of plants. I've learned a lot from her. You should repot this sad thing in dry soil. And hold the water for a day or two."

Blair scowled as Dana moved to her seat.

I'm positive Dana tries to help, Diary. It just doesn't seem like it most of the time.

For a popular girl, Dana sure knows how to get people mad at her! And it could cost her the Prom Princess contest!

Dear Diary,

I sat in the backstage lounge of the auditorium waiting for Dana. It was Ashley's idea, in case Dana needed anything before she made her speech.

I didn't think Dana would want me around for anything, but if that's what my sister wanted, fine.

When Natalie came into the lounge, I pulled out my notebook. I acted like I was studying. Otherwise, it would be too hard to pretend I didn't know she had stolen Ashley's forms.

Dana came in a few minutes later. She was wearing low-rise brown corduroys, a tan pullover sweater, and brown shoes with a low heel. The outfit gave her a serious-student-with-style look.

I walked over to Dana. "Are you all set?" I asked.

"Yeah." Dana nodded. She glanced at the note cards she was carrying. "I hope my speech isn't too long. We're not supposed to talk for more than three minutes."

"I could time your speech, if you want," I offered.

"Great!" Dana said. She glanced over at Natalie. "Let's find someplace private."

I followed Dana to the area behind the stage curtain. No one would bother us there.

I looked at my watch and waited a couple of seconds. Then I gave her the signal to start. "Right . . . now."

"Only one Prom Princess is chosen every year at White Oak," Dana began. "She's always someone who stands out from the crowd, a leader among students. There is no doubt about it – that someone is me! Who else could she possibly be?"

I rocked back in surprise. A White Oak Prom Princess definitely didn't brag!

What am I going to do? I wondered as Dana kept talking. *If Dana gives this speech, she'll lose the contest for sure.*

"Well?" Dana asked when she finished.

I glanced at my watch. "The timing is perfect, but . . ." How could I tell Dana to change her speech without getting her really mad? "You . . . uh . . . probably shouldn't say that you set *all* the trends at White Oak."

"But I do!" Dana exclaimed. "I get all the latest styles first. That's how everyone here knows what to wear."

"I know that," I said. "But so does everyone else."

"Oh, yeah." Dana nodded. "I see what you mean."

"And," I went on, "pointing out that some girls beg to sit at your table probably won't be a big vote-getter."

"Why not?" Dana asked, puzzled. "Lots of girls ask to sit with me in the dining hall."

"How many do you turn down?" I asked.

"Most of them," Dana said. Then her eyes widened. "Would they hold that against me?"

"Maybe," I said. "So why remind them?"

"Whatever." Dana looked annoyed. "Anything else?"

"Well, maybe we could make your speech about what the perfect Prom Princess should be," I said. "And just *hint* that you're the best choice."

Prom Princess

"I don't have time to write a new speech!" Dana protested.

I remembered something Dana had said to me at softball practice. "I've got an idea," I said. "Come on!"

I knew the drama teacher kept a clipboard and pen in the prop room. I pushed open the door and stepped into the dark room. I knew it was full of sets, wardrobe racks and boxes of props.

"Watch your step," I warned Dana, but it was too late.

"Ouch!" Dana cried out. "I tripped over something."

I found the light switch and flipped on the light.

"Oh, no!" Dana squealed. "I broke the heel off my shoe!"

"You can wear mine," I said. Dana glanced at me and wrinkled her nose. I was wearing a Mighty Oaks sweatshirt, jeans and black trainers. Not exactly Dana's style.

"I'd rather limp on one heel," Dana said.

"Check the wardrobe boxes," I suggested.

I reached for the clipboard on the wall. The pen was attached to it with a string. I sat on the floor and turned the note cards over to write on the blank side while Dana searched through boxes.

"This box is marked 'shoes'!" Dana said. She leaned over an upside-down bicycle to reach the boxes. "Maybe there will be something in here."

"I hope so," I said. I kept writing as Dana tried on a pair of black flats.

"They're too small," Dana complained.

I looked up and gasped. Dana's sweater was streaked with black grime from the bicycle.

Dana looked down at the black mark. She threw up her hands. "Now what am I going to do?"

Just then, I heard the sound of applause. Mrs. Pritchard's voice came over the loudspeakers. "Good evening, young ladies. I know you're all eager to hear from our Prom Princess finalists. We'll begin with Natalie Pittman."

"We have to do something!" Dana said. "I'm up in three minutes!"

"Don't panic, Dana!" I said.

I crossed my fingers behind my back and wished for luck. Because, Diary, we really needed it!

Chapter 10

Thursday

Dear Diary,

Phoebe and I had front-row, centre seats so we could tape the Prom Princess speeches.

"Showtime," Phoebe said when Natalie walked onto the stage.

"I am absolutely *thrilled* to be a Prom Princess finalist," Natalie said. She was wearing a cranberry-red skirt with a matching sweater over a T-shirt. "And so surprised!" she added.

"Sure she is," I said under my breath.

"In fact," Natalie went on, "being nominated for Prom Princess is one of the best things that's ever happened to me. It's even more exciting than when I won the school spelling bee, or that gold medal I got at the championship swim meet."

I rolled my eyes.

"But then the ideal White Oak student tries to be the best at everything she does," Natalie went on. "I know I do."

You cheat to win, Natalie! I thought. No one in the audience knew that, or seemed to care that Natalie was bragging.

"Success is built on hard work, determination, and a winning attitude," Natalie said. "For me, being Prom Princess will be a dream come true. So I'd like your vote at the Spring Prom."

The crowd applauded as Natalie left the stage.

"And now, Dana," Phoebe said. She refocused her camera.

Dana stepped onto the stage – and I couldn't believe my eyes, Diary! Dana, who always looks as if she stepped out of a fashion magazine, was wearing brown trousers with Mary-Kate's sweatshirt and black trainers.

Several girls in the audience giggled as Dana walked to centre stage. Dana just looked over the crowd and smiled. "Being Prom Princess is a thrill for every girl who has ever been chosen," Dana said. "But the crown does not belong to the winners alone."

"It doesn't?" Phoebe asked in a whisper.

I shrugged, but Dana had my attention!

"Every Prom Princess shares the honour with the girls who voted for her," Dana went on. "She wouldn't be Prom Princess without the support of her friends and fellow students. We're all a team at White Oak."

Dana struck a cheerleader's pose with her hands on her hips and her feet apart. Then she pointed to the Mighty Oaks logo on her sweatshirt. "Just like the Mighty Oaks!" she declared.

Someone in the crowd whistled. Others cheered.

"So I'm asking for your vote at the dance on Saturday," Dana said with a huge grin. "And don't forget to come to the Mighty Oaks' softball game tomorrow afternoon!"

Dana led the crowd in a White Oak cheer. She ended by yelling, "Go, Oaks!" Then she ran off the stage. Everyone applauded wildly.

"That was fantastic!" Phoebe's smile was almost as big as mine. Dana's speech was inspired!

My good feeling about Dana's chances of winning the Prom Princess contest lasted all night. I didn't have *any* doubts – until Phoebe and I started to edit our movie on Friday afternoon.

We were in the Young Filmmakers Club meeting room. We finally had a title: *The Making of a Prom Princess*. But we were having trouble finding video that we could use.

I shook my head. "We need ten minutes of video when Dana isn't being bossy, rude or stuck-up."

"Everybody loved Dana's speech," Phoebe said.

"That's only three minutes," I pointed out. "We can't have seven minutes of Dana being . . . Dana."

"Probably not," Phoebe agreed. "But Dana isn't always as mean as she sounds."

"We know that, but how many other girls do?" I asked.

"Does Dana have *any* chance to win Prom Princess?" Phoebe asked.

"I don't know," I said. "I just don't know."

Dear Diary,

I sat on the bench while the Mighty
Oaks warmed up for the game against
Mount Truman. Classes were over for the week, and everyone had turned out to cheer the team on.

Dana came into the dugout with her notebook. Her report about the game would be in tomorrow's issue of the *Acorn*.

"Hi, Dana," I said. "From what I hear, everyone thought your speech was fantastic."

"I know. Thanks," Dana said. "Did the nurse check your arm this morning?"

"Yes, it's completely healed," I said. I didn't mention that I was still benched for disobeying Coach's order not to practise – thanks to Dana!

"Well, that's good," Dana said. She sat down and opened her notebook. I turned my attention to the game.

In the first inning, a Mount Truman batter hit a high fly between first and second. Natalie was playing first base for the Mighty Oaks. The batter ran past first towards second. But Natalie left first base, too.

"Should Natalie be going for that ball?" Dana asked me.

"Not really," I said. Lexy ran in from the outfield to make the catch. Natalie caught the ball instead.

"Well, at least Natalie got the out," Dana said.

I watched as the runner going for second turned and ran safely back to first.

"But if Natalie had stayed on first, Lexy would have thrown to her," I explained. "Natalie could have tagged the runner out. Then we'd have *two* outs."

The Mount Truman team was still two runs ahead in the fourth inning. There was no one on base for White Oak when Natalie stepped up to bat.

"If Natalie can just get on base, we might tie the score this inning," I said.

"I hope you're right, Mary-Kate," Dana said.

Natalie hit a hard drive to centre field. We all

cheered her to keep going when she rounded first base.

"Watch out, Natalie!" I screamed when Natalie touched second and headed for third. The Mount Truman outfielder had her arm drawn back to throw the ball.

"Stay there!" Dana shouted when Natalie made it to third.

But Natalie raced for home. The outfielder threw to the catcher. The catcher caught the ball and tagged Natalie out before she crossed home plate.

All the Mighty Oaks in the dugout groaned.

"Why did Natalie do that?" Dana was furious. "She was safe at third!"

I had a feeling I knew why Natalie was acting this way. She had been trying to make great plays the whole game. She probably thought that would get her more Prom Princess votes.

"I wish I could be on the field helping the team," I said, mostly to myself. Dana stared at me, then smiled. I have no idea why. Mount Truman was still ahead by two runs when the Mighty

Oaks got up to bat in the last inning. The team needed three runs to win.

Dana suddenly left the dugout and talked to Coach Hadley for a few minutes. Then she sat in the bleachers with her friends.

Samantha Kramer struck out, and Kayla Bailey was tagged out at first. Lexy and Campbell both hit singles. They were on first and second with two outs when Natalie got up to bat.

Coach Hadley stopped Natalie from leaving the dugout. "Sit down, Natalie. You've been playing to make yourself look good all afternoon. We need a team player to bat for us now."

"But I—" Natalie stopped herself and sat down, frowning.

"Okay, Mary-Kate," Coach Hadley said. "You're up."

"Me?" I was surprised, but I didn't ask questions. I quickly put on the batting helmet and grabbed my bat.

"Get a homer, Mary-Kate!" Ashley yelled from the bleachers.

I just wanted a good hit so that Lexy and Campbell could score. Helping the team win was more important than my own home-run glory.

"Come on, Mary-Kate!" someone else yelled. "You can do it."

I looked up. I couldn't tell who had shouted, but Dana was giving me a thumbs-up!

Did Dana ask the coach to let me play? I wondered.

I gripped the bat. The first pitch was right across the plate. I swung and slammed the bat against the ball. It sailed towards the outfield, and I raced for first.

"It's going!" someone shouted.

"Going, going, gone!" The crowd cheered.

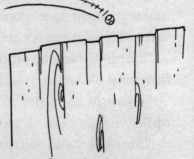

A home run! I saw the ball disappear over the fence. Lexy and Campbell scored as I ran the bases.

"Mary-Kate! Mary-Kate!" everyone chanted.

I crossed home plate to score the winning run.

White Oak had won the first game of the season!

And I had my first homer towards breaking Jamie Jerome's record.

I know I said that I hoped Dana wouldn't win the Prom Princess contest, Diary. Well, I've changed my mind.

Chapter 11

Saturday

Dear Diary,

First thing in the morning, someone
pounded on my door. "Open up,
Mary-Kate!" Ashley called.

Campbell was stretched out on her
bed, so I jumped out of my bed to open the door.
Ashley and Phoebe rushed in.

"Look at this!" Ashley
pulled a copy of the
Acorn out of her
backpack and held it up.

The headline read:
"Mighty Oaks Win!"
Right below that, it read:

"Mary-Kate on Track to Break Home-run Record!"

I took the paper from Ashley and read the
article. Dana had written about all the highlights of
the game. She even praised all the players for
trying hard and not giving up. She did not
mention that Coach Hadley had taken Natalie out
of the game.

I read the last sentence aloud: "'Mary-Kate Burke
has a good chance of breaking Jamie Jerome's
home-run record while she's still in First Form.'"

"It's hard to believe Dana wrote that," Campbell said.

"Well, Dana isn't always as mean and nasty as everyone thinks," Ashley said. "Not all the time, anyway."

Phoebe grinned. "We've got some great examples on video of Dana being brutally nice."

I couldn't imagine that Dana and I would ever be close friends. I was just happy she wasn't giving me a hard time!

And, Diary, guess what? I was even happy that I was going to vote for her!

Dear Diary,

What a day! Phoebe and I hung "Vote for Dana" posters all over campus. Some of our friends handed out flyers for her. Then we went to tape Dana getting ready for the Prom.

"I'm going to pull your hair up and back into a twist," Brooke said. "It will look elegant, and the princess tiara will fit right over it."

"*If* I win," Dana corrected.

I was totally shocked. Dana actually admitted that *not* winning was a possibility!

"I heard some girls on the softball team talking this morning," Kristen said.

"Did they like my article in the *Acorn*?" Dana asked.

"Loved it," Kristen said. "And they're upset with Natalie for almost costing them the game yesterday."

"So they're going to vote for you, Dana," Brooke said.

"Fantastic!" I said.

"Yeah," Kristen agreed. "It's still going to be close."

"I don't want to talk about it," Dana snapped. She looked at Phoebe. "No more camera, okay? Come back at seven o'clock when I'm ready to leave."

"Okay," I said. "Phoebe and I have to get dressed, too. Brent won't mind being on camera, will he?"

Brent was Dana's date. He would be waiting in the Student Union with all the boys from Harrington.

"No way," Dana said. "He's a big ham."

Mary-Kate and Campbell came to my room just as Phoebe and I finished dressing.

"Wow!" Mary-Kate exclaimed. "You guys look gorgeous!"

"Thanks!" My dress was lavender. Phoebe had braided a sprig of tiny purple flowers with purple and white ribbons into my hair. "So do you!"

Mary-Kate's dress was pale pink with sparkly straps. She wore her hair high on her head.

Campbell wore a dark green skirt with a light green top. Phoebe had found a light blue 1950s dress at a thrift shop. It was tied with a huge bow at the back.

We all went over to Phipps House to pick up Dana. Kristen and Brooke were waiting with her in the lounge. Phoebe had the camera going when Dana made her grand entrance into the Student Union. Brent was waiting for her.

"You look great, Dana!" Brent grinned.

"Thanks. Will you get me some soda, Brent?" Dana asked. "I'm so nervous, my throat is dry."

I gestured for Phoebe to pan the room. The prom theme was "Spring Garden." The whole hall was decorated with flowers, greenery, fluffy fake animals and white picket fences. Cotton clouds were hanging from the ceiling on strings. A D.J. was set up on a stage at the far end of the room.

"I see Ross and Jordan," Mary-Kate said. She nodded to our boyfriends, who were standing by the snack table.

"I already told Ross I'd be busy with my video the first part of the dance," I explained. "Will you and Jordan hang out with him until after the Prom Princess is announced?"

"No problem," Mary-Kate said. She hurried off to join her date – and mine!

Dana sat down at a table and stared nervously at the ballot box.

The large box was decorated with flowers, streamers and birds. A teacher handed out ballots and checked off names to make sure no one voted more than once.

"Get some shots of people voting, Phoebe," I directed.

"I'm on it," Phoebe said. She aimed the camera at the line of girls in front of the ballot box. She panned back to Dana's table when Blair came up.

"Thank you, Dana," Blair said. "I repotted my plant. It perked up just enough for me to get some great shots before I picked the beans."

"That's nice." Dana kept watching the ballot box.

"Wow! Look at Holly!" Phoebe trained the camera on the girl and pointed with her free hand.

I looked over. Holly was waiting in line to vote. She had taken Dana's advice, too. Her hair was short and curly. The new style *did* soften her angular face.

Holly waved her ballot when she caught my eye. *Is she voting for Dana?* I wondered.

Brent came back to Dana's table with a soda. "Come on, Dana, let's dance," he suggested.

"Good idea!" I nodded. Our video of the dance would be hopelessly dull if Dana just stared at the ballot box all night. "It'll help pass the time."

Phoebe and I caught everything on camera. We even got a shot of the teacher taking the ballot box away to count the votes.

Then – *finally* – Mrs. Pritchard walked out on stage to announce the winner of the Prom Princess contest.

I was as nervous as Dana! Would our video project be called *The Making of a Prom Princess: Winner* or *The Making of a Prom Princess: Loser*?

Chapter 12

Saturday

Dear Diary,

I rushed over to Ashley when Mrs. Pritchard walked onto the stage. Campbell, Jordan and Ross came with me. "I can't stand the suspense!" I said.

"Dana's going to win," Campbell said. "I feel it."

"I *so* hope that's true!" Ashley grinned.

Phoebe aimed the camera at the stage.

"I'd like to welcome you all to White Oak's Spring Prom," Mrs. Pritchard said. "I'm sure you're all anxious to know who this year's Prom Princess is, but first—"

A groan went through the crowd.

Dana gripped Brent's hand. Kristen and Brooke stood close behind her. Natalie smiled with her hands tightly clasped.

"Let's have a round of applause for the decorating committee!" Mrs. Pritchard clapped her hands.

The crowd's applause was polite and ended quickly. Everyone wanted to know who had won the contest!

"I'd like to thank all the teachers who helped make the Spring Prom a fabulous success," Mrs. Pritchard said. "Even the voting went smoothly."

The D.J. stepped up beside the headmistress. "And I think everyone would *really* like to know who won," he said.

"Nobody cares about *that*, do they?" Mrs. Pritchard joked. "All right. I'm happy to announce that the winner of White Oak's First Form Prom Princess contest is—"

Ashley grabbed my arm and squeezed.

"Dana Woletsky!" Mrs. Pritchard said.

Dana screamed in total surprise. Kristen and Brooke jumped up and down, squealing.

"Yes!" I yelled. I whistled and cheered and gave Ashley a high five. "We did it, Ashley! We did it!"

Ashley hugged me. "Thanks for helping."

Phoebe was excited, too, but she was still taping. She was trying not to jiggle the camera!

Brent took Dana's hand and led her onto the stage.

I looked at Natalie. She wasn't smiling any more. She ran out of the hall in tears.

"It's too bad you weren't in the Prom Princess finals, Ashley," I said. "But at least you got a happy ending."

Ashley nodded. "And I sort of made friends with Dana."

"Me too," I said, much to my own surprise.

"I'm pleased to crown Dana the Princess of the Spring Prom!" Mrs. Pritchard placed a sparkling rhinestone tiara on Dana's head. "Would you like to say a few words or thank anyone, Dana?"

"Get ready to take a bow, Ashley," Phoebe said. She looked up from the camera.

Ashley smiled and motioned for Phoebe to keep filming.

"This is so fantastic!" Dana gushed with a huge smile. "I want to thank my best friends, Kristen and Brooke, for sticking by me even though they didn't nominate me."

Kristen and Brooke took quick, embarrassed bows.

"And Mrs. Pritchard and the teachers who made the Spring Prom and the Prom Princess contest possible," Dana went on.

Mrs. Pritchard beamed. "Thank you, Dana."

"And last but not least," Dana said, "you should be very glad you voted for me. I worked really hard and totally deserve this!"

Dana took Brent's hand, and they stepped off the stage. They started to dance when the D.J. cued up a slow song.

"What?" Phoebe exclaimed. "That's it? What about thanking you two?"

Ashley and I broke out laughing.

"Oh, well," Ashley said. "She's still the same old self-centred Dana."

"Yeah." I giggled. "Some things never change."

Dear Diary,

Ashley came to my room after the last meeting of the Young Filmmakers Club today. She sat on my bed while I changed out of my softball uniform.

"How did the game go, Mary-Kate?" Ashley asked.

"We beat Bradenton," I said. "Six to three." I grinned. "And I hit a home run! My second for the season – with ten games to go."

"That is fantastic!" Ashley exclaimed.

"Thanks. How did things go with your movie?" I asked.

"Okay, I guess," Ashley answered. *"The Making of a Prom Princess* was voted the *second*-best video."

"Second?" I gasped. "That means your video won't be in the film festival."

"No." Ashley shook her head. "Blair's movie was chosen for the White Oak entry in the student category."

I blinked. "Your Prom Princess video got beaten by *The Life and Death of a Green Bean*?"

Prom Princess

Ashley shrugged. "That's showbiz."

I shook my head. "Dana won't be happy. She wanted to be discovered by Hollywood at the film festival. Now she's been bested by a green bean!"

"It's worse than that!" Ashley said. "Dana was beaten by a green bean that *she* saved with some brutally good gardening advice!"

That sent both of us into howls of laughter.

mary-kateandashley

TWO
of a kind™

Diaries

Camp Rock 'n' Roll

by Judy Katschke

HarperCollins*Entertainment*
An Imprint of HarperCollins*Publishers*

A PARACHUTE PRESS BOOK

Chapter 1

Sunday

Dear Diary,

I thought this day would never come! My twin sister, Ashley, and I are finally on the bus going to Camp Rock 'n' Roll, and the bus is already rocking!

A girl with bright orange hair across the aisle is playing a keyboard. Three girls in the back of the bus are singing at the top of their lungs. Other girls are playing guitars, tambourines, and even a violin!

Ashley is sitting right in front of me, strumming her acoustic guitar.

"Pump it up, you guys," a curly-haired girl with a trumpet shouted, "so they can hear us all the way at camp!"

You've probably figured out, Diary, that Camp Rock 'n' Roll is not a typical bug-juice-and-sports summer camp. It's a totally cool music camp for middle-school girls.

Going to Camp Rock 'n' Roll this summer was my idea. Ever since I was a little kid I've thought it would be awesome to be in a band. As soon as I showed Ashley the Camp Rock 'n' Roll brochure, she was itching to go, too.

"It says you have to bring a musical instrument to camp or know how to play one," Ashley said back at our boarding school, White Oak Academy for Girls in New Hampshire. Ashley and I are both in the First Form, which is what our school calls the seventh grade. "Hey, I can take our guitar!"

"You mean *your* guitar," I said. "You're the only one who plays it now."

Ashley and I both took guitar lessons a couple of years ago. I quit guitar to take piano lessons. Then I quit piano lessons so I could play softball.

"What instrument will you take?" Ashley asked.

"I'm not," I said. "All I want to do is sing!"

It was a no-brainer, Diary. I've already starred in two musicals at White Oak. I love everything about being onstage – belting out songs, taking bows to all that applause – even the hot stage lights and the crowded dressing room. I'm always totally happy when I'm performing.

I glanced at the girl sitting next to me. She was wearing headphones, and she'd been playing her electric guitar since we left Boston. I couldn't tell whether she was rocking out to the beat of her guitar or the music blaring from her Walkman.

"What are you listening to?" I asked her.

The girl smiled. She was wearing a black T-shirt, ripped-up jeans, and lots of leather jewellery with studs.

"It's Gag Reflex's newest CD, *Regurgitate*," she said. "Next I'm going to listen to Rodney Beecham's latest disc."

I knew all about Gag Reflex. They're a cool heavy metal band. Rodney Beecham is a superfamous British rock singer. All the radio stations play his tunes.

"I'm Mary-Kate Burke," I said.

"I'm Janelle Chow," she said. "I guess you figured out that I'm a serious metal-head."

I did notice one thing about Janelle's head: Her spiky black hair was full of green streaks.

"Is that stuff permanent?" I asked, pointing to her bright green bangs.

"It washes out," Janelle explained. "This hair dye is made out of vegetables, not chemicals."

As the bus rumbled along the highway toward Pennsylvania, Janelle and I told each other about our schools and families. Janelle is a twin like I am. She has a twin brother named Joshua, whom she says she is *nothing* like. He's a total computer geek.

"Ashley and I look alike but we're different, too," I said. "I like performing, horseback riding, and sports. Ashley likes ballet, writing, and shopping. But we both *love* music."

"Then you'll both *love* Camp Rock 'n' Roll," Janelle said. "It's totally awesome."

"How do you know?" I asked.

"I went there last year," Janelle said. "Where do you think I learned how to do *this*?"

Janelle played a lightning-fast riff on the guitar, then pumped one fist in the air. "That was *without* my amp," she said, smiling. "Wait till you hear me with juice."

Janelle started telling me all about Camp Rock 'n' Roll. "Every day we have music classes and some sporty stuff like volleyball or canoeing. But the best part of camp is the Battle of the Bands. First we're all split into bands. Then each camper has to pick an instrument to play."

"Or sing?" I asked.

"All of us get to sing," Janelle said. She went on. "The bands compete in four different rounds. In the fourth round the two bands with the highest total scores from the first three rounds compete for the title of Best Band."

"Cool!" I said.

"I wonder if Terrence 'the Terror' Boyle will be one of the judges this summer," Janelle said, almost to herself. "He's the only judge who tells it like it is."

That didn't worry me. Honesty is good when you're learning. And I want to learn everything about singing rock.

No more singing in the shower for me, Diary. Next stop, Camp Rock 'n' Roll!

Dear Diary,

Sorry for the squiggly writing, but the bus keeps hitting a ton of bumps. And the girl across the aisle keeps hitting me with the neck of her bass guitar!

So far, I *love* Camp Rock 'n' Roll – even though we're not there yet. Mary-Kate is going, and so is my best friend and school roommate, Phoebe Cahill.

Four weeks ago Phoebe's family's summer vacation plans fell through. She went into a real funk.

"What am I going to do all summer?" Phoebe wailed. "I must be the only girl at school with no plans!"

Plans? I suddenly had the perfect plan!

"Phoebe, you should come to Camp Rock 'n' Roll with me," I said. "You play guitar better than I do. And you write the most awesome songs, too."

"I'm not the rock type, Ashley," Phoebe said. "I like singing serious songs with messages. Like Jewel and Sheryl Crow. And some of the folksingers of the sixties."

I smiled at Phoebe sitting cross-legged on her bed in her tie-dyed tee and bell-bottoms. Not only did she listen to the singers of the sixties, she dressed like them, too.

No surprise there. Phoebe's closet at school is packed with vintage clothes from antique boutiques and flea markets. It's what makes Phoebe . . . Phoebe.

"Don't worry," I said. "I'm sure you can play whatever kinds of songs you want at Camp Rock 'n' Roll."

"Well . . ." Phoebe said slowly, "I don't know."

Diary, when I get an idea, I don't give up easily.

"Please, please, please come to camp with me, Phoebe!" I plopped down on the bed next to her. "We'll have so much fun playing our guitars and coming up with songs!"

"I'll think about it," Phoebe said.

I had to make Phoebe go with me. So I put pictures of Camp Rock 'n' Roll all over our dorm room. I whispered "Camp Rock 'n' Roll" into Phoebe's ear while she slept. I wrote Camp Rock 'n' Roll with the pepperoni on our pizza!

Camp Rock 'n' Roll

I wanted Phoebe to come to camp more than anything because she's like a second sister to me. We share secrets, a room at school, and – if Phoebe didn't have such a unique style – we'd share clothes. I knew I'd miss her like crazy if I had to go to camp without her.

As summer drew closer, Phoebe still couldn't decide. "What if I don't make any friends at camp?" she asked. "What if all the girls are the bubblegum-pop type? You know I don't click with them."

"Don't worry," I assured her. "I promise we'll stick together all through camp, no matter what."

"Promise?" Phoebe asked.

I drew an imaginary X on my chest and said, "Cross my heart and hope to croak. Drop an eyeball in my Coke."

"Okay," Phoebe said. "But remember: I'm going to sing thoughtful music – not that glitter and midriff stuff."

But on the bus to camp, Phoebe started to worry again.

"Ashley," she whispered. "Look at all the girls going to camp. They're all dressed so ... so ... trendy."

I looked around. The girl playing bass guitar had on a floor-length denim skirt and a camouflage tank. One girl's jacket had the word SUPERSTAR written on the back with silver studs. The girl sitting next to Mary-Kate had green hair!

I studied Phoebe in her simple white peasant blouse and faded vintage jeans. "Musicians don't have to dress a certain way," I said. "We'll have fun no matter what."

Phoebe started strumming her guitar. I was about to join in with my own when Mary-Kate tapped my shoulder.

"Ashley," she said. "I think we're here!"

I leaned over Phoebe and stared out the window. The bus passed through a gate decorated with music notes.

A bunch of college-age kids cheered the bus as it rolled onto the campgrounds. Some wore tees with the word COUNSELOR. Others had tees that read ROADIE. I knew from going to concerts that roadies set up the musical instruments and amps for their favorite bands.

The counselors and roadies circled the bus as it hissed to a stop. Then they all started to play *kazoos*!

"This *is* going to be fun!" Phoebe giggled.

I glanced back at Mary-Kate, and she gave me a big thumbs-up sign. We were at Camp Rock 'n' Roll at last!

Chapter 2

Later Sunday

Dear Diary,

I know I already wrote in you today, but I just *have* to tell you about my first day at Camp Rock 'n' Roll!

Everything about this place is cool. There's a main house and five bunks. Behind the bunks is a field for sports. (Not that you'll find *me* there, Diary.) Further down a hill is an awesome lake for swimming, canoeing, and kayaking. The camp has its own theatre, and a music building for classes and practice. There's an arts and crafts hut and a rec hall, and a mess hall for eating meals.

Here's the best part so far: Mary-Kate, Phoebe, and I are all in the same bunk.

"See?" I told Phoebe. "I told you we'd all get to be together."

Mary-Kate and I have been to lots of summer camps before, and the bunks are usually named after birds or bugs. Not at Camp Rock 'n' Roll. Here, the bunks are named after rock superstars. Ours is named Bunk Elvis.

"Elvis Presley was called the King of Rock 'n' Roll," Mary-Kate said. "So *that* means Bunk Elvis totally rules!"

Aside from the painting of Elvis on the door, our bunk looks like any other camp bunk. We have three sets of bunk beds, and each of us has her own cubby. There are two closets – one for clothes and one for musical instruments – plus a bathroom with the skinniest shower stall I ever saw.

The one single bed is for our counselor, Ivy Loomis. Ivy is a college music major and wears lots of bracelets and colourful beads in her cornrows.

Our two other bunk mates are Janelle Chow and Lark Maitland. Lark has long dark hair and big sad-looking brown eyes. Janelle is her total opposite. She has a huge smile that's about as electric as her guitar.

"Yo, dudes!" Janelle shouted, waving her guitar in the air. "Who's ready for some monster rock?"

"Not me," Phoebe murmured.

We dropped our duffel bags and instruments on the floor. I noticed one of the beds was empty.

"There's one more girl coming who didn't take the bus," Ivy explained. "Her name is Erin Verko."

"Did someone say my name?" a perky voice asked.

I spun around. A girl with long pin-straight blonde hair bounced into the bunk. She was wearing a pink halter top and black cropped pants decorated with silver zippers.

"You guys!" Erin said with a little jump. "Is music camp going to be superfun or what?"

I stared at Erin. With her cutting-edge clothes, she looked as if she had stepped right out of a fashion magazine!

"Where's your gear, Erin?" Ivy asked.

Just then three roadies entered the bunk. Two of the guys lugged duffel bags and wheeled suitcases. The third carried a long black case.

"What is all *that*?" Phoebe asked.

"Just my keyboard case," Erin said. She began to pull clothes out of a suitcase. "And a few things to wear."

"A few?" Janelle echoed. "No wonder you didn't take the bus – there wasn't enough room!"

"Exactly." Erin giggled as the guys left the bunk. I couldn't take my eyes off Erin's clothing. That's because all my life I've had a serious passion for fashion. Now, right in my own bunk, was a fellow style-freak!

"Erin, your clothes are awesome. Where do you go shopping?" I just had to ask.

"I don't. My mom's the fashion editor for *Teen Scene* magazine," Erin explained. "She gets a lot of the clothes they use in the photo shoots."

"I love *Teen Scene*!" I said. I checked out some of

the clothes on the bed. "Omigosh – these pants were on the cover of the May issue. And this jacket was in the 'Gotta Have It!' section of the April issue!"

"Dead on!" Erin said. She looked me up and down. "You look like you're about my size. You can borrow some of my clothes, if you want."

"No way!" I squealed.

"Yes, way!" Erin squealed back.

"I'm Ashley, by the way," I added.

"Shut *up*!" Erin cried. "My *middle* name is Ashley!"

"No way!" I cried.

"Start unpacking, girls," Ivy said. "There's a campfire jam tonight. You'll get to sing, play your instruments, and meet the Battle of the Bands judges."

We all chatted and laughed as we unpacked and made our beds. Only Lark didn't say much, but she grinned when Mary-Kate spread out her Chicago Cubs sheets. Phoebe made her bed like she does at school, with Indian paisley throws. I was tucking in my turquoise sheets when I heard a loud puffing noise. I turned around. Erin was sitting cross-legged on the floor, blowing up something plastic and pink.

"What's that?" I asked.

"It's my inflatable chair," Erin said. "Just because we're in the woods at camp doesn't mean we have to rough it, right?"

"Right," I agreed. I'd always wanted a chair like that for my room at school.

Erin gazed around the bunk. "Now where should I hang up my beaded curtain . . . and plug in my karaoke machine?"

I could see Phoebe roll her eyes behind her blue-frame glasses. "Erin Verko is like a breakfast cereal," she whispered to me. "Flaky!"

"You're wrong," I whispered back to Phoebe. "I think she's fun!"

Dear Diary,

Wait until you hear about the amazing campfire I just went to. Everyone showed up with an instrument. There was every kind – from a violin to drums. The only campers without instruments were Lark and me.

"Do you play an instrument, Lark?" I asked.

Lark shook her head and said, "I kind of sing."

"Really?" I said. "Me too."

Lark dropped her marshmallow as she was about to put it on her stick. She started to reach for a new one, when a counselor hurried over.

"Take this, Lark," the counselor said. She held out a crispy marshmallow on a stick. "It's already toasted."

117

Lark's face turned red. "No, thanks," she said.

The counselor looked disappointed as she walked away. I didn't get it. Why was she so eager to give Lark an already-toasted marshmallow? I was about to drop my own marshmallow to see if the same thing would happen, when –

"Welcome to Camp Rock 'n' Roll!" a voice shouted.

A woman wearing black jeans and a red tee was standing on a tree stump. I knew from her picture in the brochure that she was Stella Vickers, the camp owner. Stella used to sing with a group called Heartstrings in the late seventies.

Stella told us about the activities, then about the Battle of the Bands. "Each bunk will be split into two bands. And each band will have one lead vocalist."

That's got to be me! I thought.

"Tomorrow you'll meet your music instructors," Stella went on. "But right now I'd like you to meet our three judges, starting with the one and only Clarence Meekins!"

A tall thin guy wearing a backward baseball cap jumped up. Everyone cheered as he waved both arms.

"Next, the incredibly glam Sophie Amir!" Stella shouted. "Give it up for her, ladies!"

Sophie stood up and waved shyly as everyone cheered. She did look glam in a gold halter top and denim capris.

"And here's the guy who cannot tell a lie," Stella said. "Put your hands together for Terrence Boyle!"

A man with dark curly hair stood up. He rolled his eyes as a few kids hissed and booed. Then everyone laughed.

"Now put down your marshmallows and pick up your instruments!" Stella declared. She picked up her own guitar. "Let's kick off the night with 'Wild Thing.' If you know it, jump in. If you don't, jump in, anyway!"

The campfire crackled as we all jammed. Ashley and Phoebe strummed their guitars. Janelle leaned way back as she played some serious guitar riffs. Erin worked her keyboard, and I sang at the top of my lungs.

Every time I looked at Lark, her mouth was shut. *That's weird*, I thought. *Why doesn't she want to sing?*

We sang and played until the campfire finally fizzled out. Then Stella shouted, "You ladies have it rockin' on. Have a great night and I'll see you all tomorrow!"

Back in Bunk Elvis, Ivy switched on the light and said, "Whoa! Some lucky camper got a care package." She pointed to a large cardboard box that was sitting on Lark's bed. The return address was London, England.

"Who lives in England?" Phoebe asked.

"Just my dad," Lark answered in a small voice.

"Maybe he sent you some English toffees," I said.

"Or English biscuits," Ashley guessed.

"Or Prince William!" Erin teased.

Lark opened the box. It was filled with sweet-smelling soaps, chocolates, and a stack of top-ten CDs.

"*That's* what I call a care package!" Janelle said. "All I ever get from my folks are pretzels and socks."

Lark read the note to herself. Erin peeked over her shoulder and read it out loud: "'Lark – have a super time at camp. Love, Dad.'"

"Can I have that note, Lark?" Ivy asked. "It would be like having an autograph from – "

"It's yours," Lark cut in. Her face turned red again.

We stared at Lark as she gave Ivy the note. Then she ran into the bathroom. What was *that* all about?

Chapter 3

Monday

Dear Diary,

First thing this morning we went to 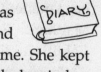 the mess hall for breakfast. Each bunk has its own table. I sat between Phoebe and Mary-Kate. Erin sat right across from me. She kept staring at Phoebe's white blouse with black spirals.

"What's the matter?" Phoebe finally asked Erin. She looked down at her blouse. "Do I have a stain somewhere?"

"No," Erin said. "My mom used to have a blouse like that. She gave it to Goodwill. Maybe it's the same one."

Uh-oh, I thought. *Wrong answer!*

"This is a vintage blouse from nineteen sixty-five," Phoebe told Erin. "I got it at Classique Boutique, not Goodwill."

"I like vintage clothes, too," Erin said. "Especially around Halloween when I want a goofy costume – "

"Waffles anyone?" I cut in.

After breakfast we collected our instruments and followed Ivy to the camp theatre.

Stella stood on the stage. "This morning we'll break up into bands," she announced as she studied a clipboard.

Phoebe stood next to me and crossed her fingers. "Please, oh, please let us be in the same one!" she whispered.

"Bunk Elvis," Stella began. "The first band will be Janelle Chow, Mary-Kate Burke, and Lark Maitland. Second band: Ashley Burke, Phoebe Cahill, and Erin Verko."

Phoebe and I let out excited little shrieks. Erin ran over to us, and we all slapped hands and jumped up and down.

After the other bands were announced, each band met their instructor. Ours was Jennifer Stanley. She had long curly black hair and a tee that read GUITAR GODDESS.

"I see we have two acoustic guitarists and a keyboard player," Jennifer said as she checked out our instruments. "What type of band would you like to be?"

"I'd like our band to be called the Songbirds," Phoebe said, her eyes shining. "And we should sing about things that are really important to kids and teens."

"Huh?" Erin said, wrinkling her nose.

"You know," Phoebe explained, "caring for the earth, being true to yourself. Our songs should have meaning."

"I don't think so," Erin said. She frowned, then snapped her fingers. "Hey, I know. Why don't we call our band something like Teen Spirit?"

"Teen Spirit," I repeated. "That name is so cool!"

"And we should sing about all kinds of fun stuff," Erin went on. "You know – boys, friends, summertime."

Diary, it was like Erin was reading my mind. Summer is my favorite season of the year. It's all about kicking back and having fun. So why not sing about it?

"What do you think?" Erin asked me.

"Are you kidding?" I exclaimed. "We love it!"

"Really?" Erin said with a little jump.

"Totally!" I replied.

"Okay, campers – I mean, rockers!" Stella called out. "Tomorrow morning you'll meet with your instructors for your first band workshop."

Erin grabbed my arm as we walked out of the theater.

"I brought some of that fake tanning spray," she said. "Maybe we can all use it when we sing about summer!"

"That's perfect!" I said.

Diary, I am so incredibly psyched. I'm in the hippest band at camp with my best friend and a cool *new* friend.

Can things get any better than that?

Dear Diary,
Here's the scoop. Janelle and I are
in the same band. So is Lark, which is
why I'm kind of bummed out.

It all started when we met our instructor, Bill
West. Bill has stringy longish hair and wire-
rimmed glasses. He had us sit in a circle on the
grass.

"Let's talk about your goals for the band," Bill
began. "How do you all see yourselves?"

"Totally in leather!" Janelle answered. "We
should jump up and down on our instruments
when we're finished playing and bite the heads off
of chocolate bunnies!"

"Are you serious?" I asked.

"Just about the leather part," Janelle said,
giggling.

"Bill?" I said and glanced at Lark. "Can our
band have two singers? I want to sing. And I think
Lark does, too."

Bill smiled at Lark, ignoring me. "Really, Lark?"
he asked. "Do you want to sing?"

"I guess," Lark said with a shrug. She didn't look
very excited. Then again, she never did.

"So we'll both sing, right?" I asked Bill.

"Sorry, Mary-Kate," Bill said. "Each band can only have one lead singer. Hey, Stella!" he yelled across the field. "It's a go! Lark is going to sing lead!"

"All-riiiight!" Stella shouted back to him.

Am I missing something? I wondered. *Lark didn't even sing at the campfire. And now she's going to sing lead?*

I looked at Lark. She was inspecting a blade of grass.

"Bill?" I said in a low voice. "Could I speak to you, please? In private?"

"Sure thing," Bill said, still smiling at Lark.

The two of us walked over to a nearby tree. "I was kind of hoping I'd get to sing," I told him. "I starred in my school musicals. I played Kim in *Bye Bye Birdie*, and I – "

"Don't worry," Bill said. "You'll definitely get to sing backup. But Stella really wants Lark to sing solo."

"Why?" I asked.

"You know how it is," Bill said with a shrug.

I *don't* know how it is, Diary. What was going on?

"Can't Lark play an instrument?" I asked. "We all had to write one down on the camp application."

"It's cool," Bill said. "We'll just give Lark a tambourine she can shake around."

I didn't get it. What was the big deal about Lark?

"Speaking of instruments, Mary-Kate," Bill said, "you wrote on your application that you play the piano. Check?"

My eyes flew wide open. Piano? I took my last piano lesson when I was ten years old. When I checked it off on the form, I never thought they'd actually make me play it.

"I did take lessons," I said slowly. "And I can read music."

"Cool!" Bill said. "We'll get you a keyboard tomorrow, and you can start jamming."

"A keyboard?" I echoed.

"It'll be perfect for the band," Bill said. "If you play piano, you'll be able to ace the keyboard in no time."

"C-c-cool," I stammered.

But it really wasn't.

I still wanted to sing lead. And how could I tell Bill that the only song I'd learned to play on the piano was "Itsy Bitsy Spider"?

Chapter 4

Tuesday

Dear Diary,

Last night in the rec hall the three of us got busy coming up with a name for our band.

"Okay," Janelle said, looking down at her notepad. "So far we've got The Diva Dollz, In Your Face, and Hangnail. Which one will it be?"

I thought about each name. Hangnail sounded painful. And In Your Face made us sound too tough. So –

"The Diva Dollz!" Lark and I said at the same time. We looked at each other and grinned.

"Diva Dollz," Janelle repeated. "It's a little girly-girl . . . but I think I like it."

So, Diary, we're The Diva Dollz.

Our first band practise in the music building came right after breakfast. Janelle, Lark, and I met Bill in Room 5. The room was packed with counselors. I even saw our counselor, Ivy, in a corner.

"Why are all the counselors here?" I whispered to Janelle.

"They're probably here to see Lark," Janelle whispered back.

I was about to ask why, when Bill walked over.

"I got you a keyboard, Mary-Kate," Bill said. He pointed to a shiny red keyboard on the side of the room.

"Great!" I said. Would I remember *anything* from those piano lessons? Feeling a little sick, I went over to the keyboard to check it out.

"Janelle, you can plug in your guitar in the corner amp," Bill explained. "Lark, stand behind this microphone. Is it the right level?" He adjusted the stand. "Or is this better?" he asked, adjusting it again.

"Anything is fine," Lark said.

Bill handed Lark a silver tambourine. She gave it a little shake. The counselors went wild.

"Work it, Lark!"

"You got it rockin', girl!"

This is so weird! I thought. *The whole camp is treating Lark as if she's the best thing since Velcro!*

I stood behind the keyboard and tapped on a few keys. There was no sound.

"You forgot to turn it on," Janelle whispered.

"Whoops," I said, flicking the on switch.

"We'll start with you, Janelle," Bill said. "Let's see what you can do."

Janelle slid to her knees and worked her electric guitar. She was amazing!

"Nice," Bill said. "We'll need to work on your chord changes and practice some new techniques."

Then Bill turned to me and said, "Let's hear what you've got, Mary-Kate. Give me a dominant seventh chord."

Seventh what? I forced a smile as I stretched my fingers. Then I began to play "Itsy Bitsy Spider."

"You're a joker, Mary-Kate." Bill chuckled. "Come on. Let's hear you play that chord."

My heart pounded. I had to play something. But there was only one song I remembered how to play.

I stretched my arms over my head. I cracked a few knuckles. Then I began to play . . . "Itsy Bitsy Spider."

When I was done I slowly looked up. Lark and Janelle were staring at me with wide eyes. So was Bill.

"Are you serious, Mary-Kate?" Bill said. He scratched the top of his head. "Is that all you know how to play?"

"I took my last piano lesson when I was ten," I confessed. "I quit to play softball."

"Softball?" Bill said. "Mary-Kate, you can't play 'Itsy Bitsy Spider' in a rock band!"

"I think I can play 'London Bridge,' too!" I blurted out. "Or 'Mary Had A Little Lamb.'"

Bill buried his face in his hands. He looked up and took a deep breath. "Is there any other instrument you can play, Mary-Kate?" he asked.

"Why do I have to play an instrument?" I asked. "I can sing!"

"Camp Rock 'n' Roll is all about learning new things," Bill explained. "Besides, everyone here should know how to play at least one instrument."

Except Lark, I thought.

It wasn't fair, Diary. But if I really wanted to stay at Camp Rock 'n' Roll, I had to play something!

I played the recorder in third grade, I thought. *Or was it a slide-whistle?*

Suddenly I remembered something else. . . .

Dad plays the saxophone, I thought. *He's always showing Ashley and me how to play a few tunes!*

"My dad showed me how to play the saxophone," I said quickly.

"Sax, huh?" Bill said doubtfully.

Janelle stepped forward. "I can add some electric riffs to Mary-Kate's parts," she said. "To juice it up."

Bill seemed to think about it. Then he smiled and said, "Check. I'll dig up a sax and some reeds, Mary-Kate. Then tomorrow we'll hear you play."

"Check!" I said, crossing my fingers behind my back.

Bill turned to Lark and smiled his biggest smile. "Lark, we're ready for you," he said. "But only if you're ready for us."

"Ready," Lark said.

Three roadies raced over to adjust Lark's mike. One offered her a bottle of water.

The room became so quiet, you could hear a guitar pick drop. Lark gripped the mike with both hands and sang a pretty song that had a good beat. Her voice was sweet and clear and very soft. But as I watched Lark I noticed something. She didn't sing with any spirit. She seemed sad, like she wished she didn't have to sing.

Still, when Lark finished, all the counselors cheered and clapped, as if she were some kind of rock star.

That does it! I turned to Janelle and whispered, "What's the deal? Why does everybody treat Lark like she's royalty?"

Janelle stared at me. "Don't you know?" she asked.

"Know what?" I asked.

"Lark's dad is Rodney Beecham!" Janelle whispered.

I stared at Janelle. Did I hear right? Did she just say Rodney Beecham?

"You mean the rock superstar with fifty gold records?" I squeaked. "The one who lives in a medieval castle?"

"That's the guy," Janelle said.

"Whoa!" I gasped.

Diary, no wonder Lark is treated like royalty. She's a princess, all right. A *rock* princess!

Dear Diary,

Wait until you find out how much Erin and I have in common!

"You mean you live in Chicago?" Erin squealed. "I live about half an hour outside of Chicago! I went into the city just last month for the big 4You concert."

I gave a little shriek. 4You is my favorite band. Mary-Kate's, too. "Are you a 4You fan?" I asked Erin.

"Are you kidding?" Erin said. "I know all of the guys' signs. Trent is an Aquarius. Matt is a Gemini. And David is – "

"Taurus," I cut in. "But he's on the cusp of – "

"Gemini!" Erin squealed.

All this happened last night in the rec hall. Phoebe stayed in the bunk to write letters, but Erin and I were busy finding out all about each other.

Here's the best part: When we got back to the bunk, Erin gave me a 4You CD that I don't have, their live concert in Japan!

Diary, I am so lucky. Not only did I come to camp with my sister and my best friend, but I made a new friend who's practically my soul mate.

I was so psyched about being in a band with Erin and Phoebe that I couldn't wait for our first practise session. It came right after a class on reading musical notes.

Jennifer listened to each of us sing. Then she made a decision.

"You all sing great," Jennifer said. "But Erin has the strongest voice, so she should sing lead."

"Yes!" Erin cheered.

"Ashley and Phoebe, you'll both play guitar and sing backup," Jennifer said. "How's that?"

I was more excited about playing my guitar than singing. And I knew Phoebe wanted to write songs more than anything.

"I'm cool with it," I said, nodding.

"Me too," Phoebe said.

"Great!" Jennifer said with a smile. "Okay, Teen Spirit. Let's start practising!"

While Erin practiced her keyboard, Jennifer taught Phoebe and me a technique called "hammer-ons."

That's when you tap on the guitar strings while you play. Then Jennifer told us that we had to choose a song to perform.

"You can pick a song from a CD," Jennifer told us, "or write one of your own."

"Ta-daaa!" Phoebe said as she ran to her guitar case. "I wrote a song for us last night."

So that's what Phoebe was doing in the bunk last night, I realized. *She was writing a song.*

"It's called 'The Lonely Beach,'" Phoebe said, holding up a sheet of paper.

"'The Lonely Beach,'" Erin said thoughtfully. Her eyes lit up. "Is it about a beach party that gets rained out?"

Phoebe shook her head. "It's about saving our beaches by protecting the environment," she explained.

Erin blinked her long blonde eyelashes. "That is so intense!" she said. "But when I think beach, I think clambakes, beach volleyball, and cute suntanned guys."

"Excuse me," Phoebe said, "but serious singers do not sing about clambakes."

"And rock stars don't sing about rotting driftwood!" Erin shot back. She wrinkled her nose. "Ewwww!"

Phoebe looked straight at me. "Ashley?" she whispered. "What do you think?"

Me? I was thinking about all those clambakes, beach volleyball games, and cute suntanned hotties –

Jennifer's voice interrupted my thoughts. "Why don't we try singing Phoebe's song?" she asked. "All bands should be open to new ideas."

Erin blew her long blonde bangs away from her forehead. "Okay," she said. "Whatever."

Jennifer ducked out of the room for a minute and came back with three copies of "The Lonely Beach." After studying the lyrics, we spent the next hour coming up with a tune.

"Let's try it!" Jennifer told us.

Erin played a few chords. Then she began to sing. . . .

"'I know a beach somewhere – hey, baby, baby – a beach where nobody cares – hey, baby, baby – '"

"Stop!" Phoebe exclaimed. She raised an eyebrow at Erin. "'Hey, baby, baby'? That's not in my song!"

"Bands should be open to new ideas," Erin said with a little grin. "Right?"

"I guess," Phoebe said, but she didn't sound happy about it.

It was obvious that Phoebe and Erin were on different pages. *They'll work it out,* I told myself. And I had to admit – I liked the "hey, baby, baby's."

It took a few tries, but we played Phoebe's song from beginning to end. I couldn't believe how good we sounded. Before we knew it, our first practice session was over.

"Great job, Teen Spirit!" Jennifer said. "We'll meet tomorrow, same time, same place."

Erin stayed behind to pack up her keyboard. Phoebe and I left the music building together.

"Aren't you totally psyched that we're playing your song, Phoebe?" I asked.

"*My* song?" Phoebe cried. "Erin just turned my endangered beach into spring break!"

"She just tweaked it a little," I said.

"*Ruined* is more like it," Phoebe muttered. "And the name 'Teen Spirit' sounds like some dippy perfume."

I stopped walking and stared at Phoebe. "If you didn't like the name, why didn't you say so?" I asked.

"Because you spoke for both of us!" Phoebe said.

I stared at Phoebe as she walked away. I *had* spoken for us both. But I'd honestly thought Phoebe liked the name.

I wish I could make Phoebe feel better about our band, I thought. *But how?*

I heard giggling and looked up. A country-rock band called The Corral Chicks was coming out of a small cabin. The girls were all wearing Western-style costumes.

"Yee-haaa!" one of them shouted.

They strutted away and I peeked inside. Shelves and racks were filled with all kinds of costumes and outrageous hats. A counselor was draping a black velvet cape on a plastic hanger. She looked up at me and smiled.

"This is the wardrobe cabin," she said. "Do you need costumes for your band?"

"Not yet, thanks," I answered.

I couldn't stop staring at the costumes.

Wow! I thought. *This is just like the drama department's costume room back at White Oak. The one Phoebe and I work in for all the plays.*

That's when I had the most amazing idea. . . .

Every band has a stylist. And Phoebe is great at costume design, I thought. *She'd have tons of fun planning Teen Spirit's look!*

And if Phoebe's happier, the whole band will be happier. Diary, why didn't I think of this before?

Chapter 5

Wednesday

Dear Diary,

This morning after breakfast, Bunk
Elvis went straight to arts and crafts.
Even the art projects here are all about
rock. Some of us silk-screened tees with the logos of
classic rock groups like The Who and Blue Oyster
Cult. Others jazzed up their own clothes with
sequins and studs.

I added some studs to a fake leather bracelet.
Lark sat next to me, wrapping red ribbons around
her tambourine.

"Do you really live in a castle, Lark?" I asked.

Lark didn't even look up. "In other words," she
said, "you want to know all about my dad."

"Not really," I said. "I want to know about *you*."

"That's a switch," Lark said. "Most kids want to
be friends with me because my dad is Rodney
Beecham. Then they lose interest when I tell them I
hardly ever see my dad."

"You don't?" I asked. "How come?"

"My mom and dad are divorced," Lark said.
"I've lived with my mom in New Mexico since I
was three. The only time my dad shows up is when
he's doing a concert in Santa Fe."

"I didn't know that," I said. "But I want to be good friends with you no matter who your dad is."

Lark gave me a smirk. "Yeah, right."

"It's true!" I insisted. "We're in the same band, right? So we have to be tight!"

Lark sighed. "I'm sorry you got bumped from singing, Mary-Kate," she said. "It's because of my dad."

"What do you mean?"

"A cable station is taping a Rodney Beecham special," she explained. "Dad's publicity guy came up with the idea of us singing together in the show. So Dad let Stella know he wanted me to practise singing lead. He said he might even perform with our band in the Battle of the Bands."

"Wow!" I exclaimed. "How cool is that?"

"Not for me," Lark admitted. "It's not as if Dad thought of the idea himself. It's, like, he's only interested in me when it helps his career. If my dad knew me better, he'd know that I don't even like singing in public. He doesn't even know what I like to do."

No wonder Lark doesn't look happy when she sings, I thought.

"Here," I said, giving Lark my leather bracelet. "Consider this a friendship bracelet. And it has nothing to do with your dad!"

Lark slipped the bracelet on and smiled. "Thanks, Mary-Kate," she said. "Maybe it'll bring me luck."

"What kind of luck?" I asked.

"Even though I don't want to sing on TV, I still want to do a good job," Lark admitted. "Maybe then my dad will want to spend more time with me."

"You'll be great, Lark," I said. "You have a beautiful voice. Just keep singing the way you always do."

I could use some of my own luck, Diary. The first round – the harmony round – is this weekend, and I have to show Bill that I can play the saxophone!

Dear Diary,

Right after lunch I called a Teen Spirit meeting down at the lake. The three of us sat beneath a big leafy tree.

"Why are we here?" Erin asked. She nodded at Phoebe's guitar and giggled. "To sing 'Kumbaya'?"

"I happen to like 'Kumbaya,'" Phoebe said.

"Listen up, Teen Spirit," I said. "It's time we talked about what our band's going to wear."

"You mean costumes?" Phoebe asked.

My plan was already working. Phoebe's face was lighting up like the Fourth of July!

"Costumes are *exactly* what I mean," I said. "Music isn't just about music anymore – it's about image."

"What if we wear all black?" Phoebe suggested. "Maybe black velvet with lots of silver jewellery."

"Sounds good," I agreed.

"Sure." Erin groaned. "If you're playing classical music."

Phoebe frowned. "What do you mean by that?"

Erin stood up. "Black and silver just sounds a little . . . formal. And serious. When I think of Teen Spirit, I think fresh eye-popping color. I think . . . pink!"

"Pink?" Phoebe repeated.

"I think everything we wear should be pink," Erin explained. "Pink tees, pink pants, flip-flops – "

I smiled as I pictured the band all pinked-out. Pink is one of my favorite colors.

"Even better, let's forget the name 'Teen Spirit,'" Erin went on. "We need something edgier. Something that tells the whole world who we are. Something like, Electric Pink."

"We could wear pink makeup, too," I said, jumping up. "Pink blush, lipstick, eye shadow – "

"We could even give ourselves pink pedicures!" Erin said. "And I think you should go electric, Ashley."

"You mean play an electric guitar?" I asked.

Erin nodded. "It goes with our image."

I liked the idea of me all in pink playing electric guitar. I held up my hand to high-five Erin.

"What do you think, Phoebe?" I asked.

Phoebe stared at me long and hard. She finally blinked and said, "You've *got* to be kidding."

"Here we go." Erin sighed.

"We're a band – not cartoon characters!" Phoebe said. "I didn't even bring pink clothes. The only pink outfit I own is a coat from the nineteen fifties. And that's back home in San Francisco!"

"I'm sorry you don't like my idea, Phoebe," Erin said. "But Ashley does. I guess you're outnumbered."

Phoebe shot me a look. "Ashley?" she said.

My stomach flip-flopped. I was in the middle again!

"Um . . ." I said. "Maybe we can wear Phoebe's silver jewellery with the outfits?" I smiled at Phoebe.

"As long as the jewellery has pink beads," Erin said.

Phoebe groaned. She picked up her guitar and walked away. I could almost see steam coming out of her ears.

"What planet is she from, anyway?" Erin asked.

"She's just – " I started.

"Never mind. It's not important," Erin said. Then she walked down to the lake to skim stones.

That was mean, I thought. But what could I do?

142

Phoebe and Erin were so different. They might never agree on anything. And as for me . . .

Diary, can I help it if I like Erin's ideas more than Phoebe's? But now I feel totally trapped between my old friend and my new friend. Why does it have to be this way, Diary? Why can't we all just get along?

Chapter 6

Thursday

Dear Diary,

As of today, the group formerly known as The Diva Dollz is Xtreme! The name change was Janelle's idea.
She said whenever she heard "Diva Dollz," she thought of a bunch of big-eyed dolls with stringy hair and giant feet.

And, as of last night, I started practising on a borrowed sax. Well, sort of. I've mostly been trying to remember where my fingers should go.

"What do you think?" I asked Ashley after practicing in the bunk. "Do I sound like Kenny G?"

"More like Lisa Simpson!" Ashley said with a giggle. "But not bad, Mary-Kate. Not bad!"

This morning after breakfast I ran back to the bunk to practice more. Janelle came, too. She wanted to look for her lucky guitar pick.

"Eww," Janelle said as I played.

I looked up. "Am I that bad?"

"It's not your playing," Janelle said. "I was just thinking of all the campers who must have spit into that thing by now."

"Gross. I never thought of that," I said. "I'd better wash the mouthpiece in soap and water."

"No good." Janelle shook her head. "Brass instruments need to be cleaned with a special kind of polish."

Janelle ran out of the bunk and was back a few minutes later with a jar of polish. "I borrowed this from Stella," she said. "Rub it all over the sax until it shines."

I opened the jar and dipped a paper towel into it. Then I rubbed the mouthpiece hard.

"It's a saxophone, not a magic lamp," Janelle said, giggling. "Come on or we'll be late for practice."

I quickly packed the sax into its case. Then Janelle and I raced to the music building. Bill and Lark were already inside.

"Before we talk about your first song, I want to hear Mary-Kate play the sax," Bill said.

"Right," I said. I slipped in a new reed. I held the sax with both hands and rested it on my right hip. I put the mouthpiece between my lips and blew a note. Suddenly the grossest taste exploded through my whole mouth!

I felt my whole face scrunching up like a raisin. I tried to keep playing, but the sour taste was too horrible!

"Are you okay, Mary-Kate?" Bill asked.

"Pleeegh!" I cried, pulling the sax away. I stuck

my tongue out and sputtered, "Phew, phew, phhhhhew! Yuck!"

"Uh-oh," Janelle said. "I think you were supposed to wipe the polish off, Mary-Kate."

"Now you tell me," I said, still sputtering.

Everyone waited while I scrubbed the waxy polish off the mouthpiece. Then Bill said, "Shall we try again?"

I gripped the sax and began to play. The sour taste was gone. But not the sour notes.

"Didn't you say you took sax lessons?" Bill asked.

"It's been a while," I confessed. "And now every time I play a note, I think about that nasty taste!"

Bill ran his hand through his hair. "Do the best you can." He sighed. "I think you'll get the hang of it soon."

Bill gave me a lesson and showed me where all the notes were. I played the sax for the rest of the practice session, but I couldn't stop tasting that gross taste. By the time practice was over, I hated playing the saxophone!

I decided I *had* to find another instrument to play in the band. But I wasn't going to tell Bill until I found it.

"Ashley," I said later, "I need your help."

Ashley was alone in the bunk. She was sitting on her bed and practicing chords on a brand-new electric guitar.

"Watch what Jennifer taught me," Ashley said. "It's called bending."

Ashley bent the guitar strings as she played. It made a really neat wailing sound.

Her acoustic guitar was leaning against the bed. I picked it up and said, "Remember when I used to play this?"

"Yeah, you were pretty good," Ashley said.

"You just gave me the most awesome idea!" I said. I sat down beside her. "If you'll give me some brushup lessons, I can play the guitar in my band."

"What?" Ashley squeaked. "Mary-Kate, learning to play an instrument takes lots of practice."

"It will all come back to me when I start to play," I explained. "I just need to go over the basics so I can fake it while I sing backup. Please, Ashley? Pleeeeeeease?"

"Okay," Ashley finally said. "But just the basics."

Ashley was a great teacher. She showed me how to play minor and major chords. Most of it *did* come back as I practiced. I thought I sounded pretty good, too.

"You're the best, Ashley." I imitated Rodney

Beecham, raising my fist. "Now I'm all ready to roooock!"

I left Bunk Elvis and found Bill coming out of the music building. He looked surprised to see the guitar. "Why didn't you tell me you play guitar, Mary-Kate?"

"You didn't ask," I said with a grin.

Diary, I've been practicing ever since, and I already have something to show for it. Perfect chord changes – and a honking blister on the middle of my thumb. Ouch!

Diary, today was the absolute worst!

It was the first day Phoebe, Erin, and I showed up at band practice as Electric Pink. Erin wore a pink miniskirt, pink tank, pink flip-flops, and the pinkest lip gloss I've ever seen. I wore pink painter's pants, a rose-colored tube top, and my pink ballet flats.

The only one not pinked-out was Phoebe. She showed up in a red-and-white-checked blouse and red shorts.

"We were supposed to wear pink," Erin said.

Phoebe folded her arms over her chest. "I told you I didn't bring any pink clothes," she said.

"But red and white makes pink!" I put in quickly.

Phoebe and Erin stopped arguing once we began jamming. The Lonely Beach song sounded great.

After practice we headed back to Bunk Elvis to drop off our instruments. Our other bunk mates weren't there, but our laundry bags were. The camp sends out our dirty laundry every Wednesday and returns it clean the next day.

Phoebe opened her laundry bag and gasped. She started yanking out her clothes. "My light-colored clothing!" she wailed. "It all came back pink!"

We dumped Phoebe's clothes on her bed. Sure enough, they were all different shades of pink.

"Here's the culprit," I said, picking up one bright red sock. "Red stuff washed in hot water usually runs."

"I didn't put that sock in there!" Phoebe said, staring at the sock. "I don't even have red socks!"

"Look on the bright side," Erin said and giggled. "Now you'll have plenty of pink clothes for the band!"

Phoebe whirled around and pointed at Erin. "You did this, didn't you?" she demanded. "Because I didn't have any pink clothes. It was your idea of a joke!"

Erin stared at Phoebe with her big blue eyes.

Then she stuck her chin out and said, "I did nothing of the kind!"

"Then who did?" Phoebe demanded.

Erin started out of the bunk. "I'm out of here," she called over her shoulder. "See you later, *Ashley.*"

"Why didn't you say something?" Phoebe asked me. "It's obvious Erin put that red sock in my wash."

"She said she *didn't,* Phoebe," I reminded her.

"And you believe her?" Phoebe asked.

"Yes, I do," I said. "Why don't you just let it go?"

"Let it go?" Phoebe cried. "There you go again, taking Erin's side. Just because you think she's so cool!"

Diary, I couldn't believe what was happening. I've seen Phoebe mad before – but never at me.

"I'm not taking sides, Phoebe!" I protested.

"Yeah, right." Phoebe turned away and started sorting her pink laundry.

The truth is, Diary, I really did believe Erin.

It's only the first week of camp, I told myself. *Phoebe and Erin will calm down, and things will get better.*

Chapter 7

Friday

Dear Diary,

The first round of the Battle of the Bands is tomorrow, and I think I'm ready. At practice this morning I knew

all the notes across the fret board and parts of our song, too.

Janelle lent me her lucky guitar pick. She'd caught it at a Gag Reflex concert, which is why it's lucky.

This morning we picked out our outfits for the first performance. Janelle chose baggy camouflage pants and a tuxedo jacket. I picked out a studded jean miniskirt and a black velvet blazer. Lark says she's going to wear her own jeans and a plain grey tank top.

"I don't want to stand out," Lark explained.

After lunch I sat on the back step of our bunk and stared out at the rolling green hills. That's when I saw it – a lone football lying on the field.

If there's just one problem about Camp Rock 'n' Roll so far, it's this: I'm going through serious sports withdrawal! Most kids here would rather play their instruments than a good game of softball.

I know this is a music camp, I thought. *But even*

Madonna played softball once. So what if it was in a movie?

I jogged over to the ball and dribbled it across the grass. I pulled my right foot all the way back to shoot it across the field. Just as I was about to kick, another foot appeared out of nowhere to hook the ball.

My jaw dropped open when I saw it was Lark's.

"Your goal is that tree behind you," she said with a grin. "Mine is the boulder across the field."

"First one to score three goals takes the match," I said, grinning back.

In no time Lark and I were into our game. I thought my football skills were pretty good, but they were no match for Lark's. She had the best fakes and speed dribbling I've ever seen. She shot the ball like a pro, and her footwork was totally awesome!

"Where did you learn to play like that?" I asked when, about ten minutes later, Lark scored her third goal.

"I've always loved football," Lark said. "Ever since I was a little kid."

As we set up for another match, Lark told me about her soccer team at home. "Most of the time I'm the goalie, but what I really like is playing forward," Lark explained. Her whole face glowed as she talked about soccer. For the first time since camp started, Lark looked happy. *Really* happy!

"I didn't think rock princesses were into sports," I joked. "I thought they spent all their time backstage at concerts, fashion shows, music awards – "

"Not this rock princess," Lark cut in. "My life with my mom is just like everybody else's. Which is why I want to be treated like everybody else."

"You are," I said. "I'll bet half the kids here don't even know you're Rodney Beecham's daughter."

"Lark, I've been looking for you!" Another girl was running toward us. It was Katie Lund, from Bunk Tina Turner.

"Maybe Katie wants to play, too," I said.

Katie stopped in front of Lark. She held out a pen. "Can you please sign my sneaker?" Katie asked.

"You want me to sign your sneaker?" Lark said. "Why?"

"Du-uh!" Katie giggled. "Because you're Rodney Beecham's daughter, that's why!"

Lark shot me an I-told-you-so look.

She looked totally miserable as she signed Katie's sneaker. It's clear she's not happy at Camp Rock 'n' Roll.

Maybe Lark would have been happier in another camp, Diary. *football* camp!

Dear Diary,

Today in practice, Phoebe, Erin, and I ran through our song three times.

"Way to go!" Jennifer cheered after our third run-through. "You guys are in perfect harmony."

If only we were in perfect harmony all the time, I thought a little sadly.

Jennifer wished us luck on the first round. Then she left for an instructors meeting.

"We should keep on practising for tomorrow," I said.

"Good idea," Phoebe agreed.

"I have a better idea," Erin said, smiling slyly. "Let's spy on the other bands."

"Spy? That is so immature," Phoebe said.

I had a bad feeling that another feud was coming on soon.

"I'm sure Erin doesn't mean *spy*," I said quickly. "She probably means we should get an idea of what we'll be up against tomorrow. Right, Erin?"

"Right," Erin said. "It'll be superfun!"

"Come on, Phoebe," I said.

Camp Rock 'n' Roll

The three of us left our instruments in the music building. We walked across the campgrounds. I heard music coming from one of the bunks. We followed the sound to Bunk Elton John and peeked through a window. The girls from a group called Stringz were practising. They were playing a cello, a fiddle, and an electric violin. Their song sounded like a rock 'n' roll version of something I'd heard before.

"That song is called 'Greensleeves,'" Phoebe whispered. "They say King Henry VIII wrote it for his true love, Anne Boleyn."

"Before or after he chopped off her head?" Erin whispered.

"You mean you actually know history?" Phoebe asked Erin. "I'm impressed."

I watched Stringz play. The song was hundreds of years old, but they made it sound totally hot. I never knew string instruments could rock like that.

Erin giggled. "Wouldn't it be funny if somebody greased their bows before the first round? So that when they started playing – zing – the bows would fly out of their hands!"

"Ha!" I laughed. Then I clapped my hand over my mouth.

Stringz stopped playing. We ducked just before they looked in our direction.

"Is somebody there?" one girl called.

Still ducking, the three of us scurried away. Erin and I were giggling. Phoebe was not.

"I can't believe what you said, Erin," Phoebe said. "About greasing their bows."

"I was just kidding!" Erin exclaimed.

"Really?" Phoebe asked. "Just like when you put the red sock into my – "

"You guys!" I had to stop them before they started arguing. "What do you want to do next – practise? Hang out?"

"Practise," Phoebe said.

"Practise can wait," Erin said. "We still have to check out The Corral Chicks. And Venus. And Fresh Start."

"No way!" Phoebe said. "We need to practise."

This time I was *not* going to be in the middle.

"Do what you want," I said. "*I'm* going back to the bunk to write a letter to my dad."

I felt Erin and Phoebe watch me as I headed toward Bunk Elvis. It was the first time I hadn't taken sides. Would they both be mad at *me* now?

Mary-Kate was in the bunk when I walked in. She was sitting on the floor, playing her guitar.

"Ashley, check it out," Mary-Kate said. "I can play Dad's favourite song, 'Stairway to Heaven.'"

I sat on the floor and hugged my knees to my chest. "At least someone is having a good time," I said.

I told Mary-Kate about Phoebe and Erin. "I want to be friends with both Phoebe *and* Erin," I explained. "But I'm always in the middle of their arguments."

Mary-Kate raised an eyebrow. "Didn't you promise Phoebe you'd stick with her all through camp?" she asked.

"Yeah," I said slowly.

Mary-Kate gave me a little smile. "So?" She looked down at her guitar and continued playing.

I kind of knew what Mary-Kate was saying. I *did* promise to stick by Phoebe, no matter what. But why did that seem to mean I couldn't be friends with Erin?

Chapter 8

Saturday

Dear Diary,

Last night I had a dream about the first round of the Battle of the Bands but woke up before I could find out who won. Bummer. Especially since today is the day.

Everyone was totally stoked at breakfast. Then we all ran back to our bunks to change into our costumes.

I was good to go in my velvet jacket and studded skirt. Janelle had on her baggy pants and tux jacket. And the streaks in her hair were bright blue!

"It's called Blueberry Blaze," Janelle said. "Don't you guys want to jazz up your hair with a little colour?"

"Um . . . I'll pass," I said with a smile.

"I just want the rounds to be *over*," Lark said.

The three of us walked to the camp theatre. As soon as we got inside, I saw the judges. Clarence and Sophie were chatting. Terrence was busy studying some papers.

"He doesn't look happy," I whispered to Janelle.

"Does he *ever*?" Janelle whispered back.

We sat down on the hard wooden theatre seats. I saw Ashley and waved. She waved back and mouthed, "Good luck!"

The roadies were onstage setting up drums and a keyboard. On the floor were cables for the mikes and amps.

Stella Vickers walked up to the center microphone. "Let's kick off the harmony round with Fresh Start," she said. "Show us what you got, girls!"

Fresh Start climbed onstage. They were all wearing low-rise pants and patterned tops. One girl had a trumpet. After a sound-check, they began to play.

The trumpet-girl took turns playing and rapping. Another girl played keyboards, and a third played drums. She banged the drums so fast, her hands were a blur!

"Give it up for Fresh Start!" Stella cheered. "Now let's see what our judges thought. Clarence?"

"Ain't it funky now?" Clarence exclaimed. "The drums were a little heavy, but the rest was cool. Way cool."

"For me, too," Sophie said. "As the first band, you were under a lot of pressure, but you handled yourself like real pros. Bravo!"

The judges were being fair. At least that's what I thought before we got to Terrence. . . .

"Fresh Start?" Terrence said mockingly. "For a band called Fresh Start, you sounded a bit stale to me."

Fresh Start's smiles vanished.

"You need to slow down a bit, too," Terrence said. "At times that trumpet sounded like a machine gun!"

Fresh Start sulked off the stage. They scored a six out of a possible ten. Not bad. Not great either.

"Did you bring my lucky guitar pick?" Janelle asked.

"Yeah, why?" I said.

"We're going to need all the luck we can get!"

Next up were The Corral Chicks in their denim Western gear. Two of them played guitar, and one played rhythm on an old-fashioned metal washboard.

"Had I known you had a washboard, I would have brought my dirty socks," Terrence told them. "And I could tell you were nervous," he went on, "just by the way you played."

The Corral Chicks scored five out of ten.

I saw Lark from the corner of my eye. Talk about nervous! She was trembling so hard, her tambourine shook.

"Next band up is Xtreme!" Stella announced.

That's us! I thought, my heart pounding.

Bill gave us a thumbs-up sign, and we hurried up onto the stage. One roadie helped Janelle plug her guitar into an amp, but about five roadies helped adjust Lark's mike.

I gazed into the audience and saw Ashley. She was giving me two thumbs-ups. I looked at Terrence. He was sipping a cup of coffee with a bored look on his face.

The roadies ran off the stage and the audience became quiet. Janelle played the first few chords. Lark began to sing in a shaky voice. That was my cue to start strumming.

Come on, lucky pick, I thought. *Don't let me down!*

After a few riffs I felt the music start to take over. I forgot about everything except playing and how good that felt. Just as I was totally rocking out, the guitar pick bounced off the strings and flew out of my hand. I froze as the pick made a splash landing in Terrence's coffee cup!

Lark stared at me with wide eyes.

"So much for lucky picks," Janelle mumbled.

Terrence fished out the wet pick. "I take my coffee with sugar and a little cream," he said. "Not guitar picks."

"S-s-sorry," I stammered.

Stella smiled at me and said, "Start again, Xtreme. And try fingerpicking this time, Mary-Kate."

We started from the top. I began to relax as I plucked the melody with my fingers. When I glanced at Janelle, her knees were bent and her head was bobbing back and forth.

I've got to pump it up, too, I thought.

I remembered the bending technique Ashley showed me. I wondered if it would work on an acoustic guitar. I bent the string and – POP – it broke!

Oh, noooo! I thought.

I held up my busted guitar. The broken string waved back and forth like undercooked spaghetti on a fork!

Janelle stopped playing. Lark stopped singing.

"What we have here is an Xtreme disaster," Terrence said. "*Two* extreme disasters in a row."

"Broken strings can happen to any guitarist, Mary-Kate," Stella called out. "Do you want to go on?"

"W-w-with what?" I stammered.

One of the roadies ran over to me. He handed me an acoustic guitar. Xtreme started again. This time we got through the whole song without a hitch.

Camp Rock 'n' Roll

"You got off to a rocky start but proved you can come back," Sophie said. "Well done, Xtreme."

"Way to go," Clarence agreed.

I looked at Terrence. He shrugged with one shoulder and finally said, "Lark was a bit nervous. Janelle's guitar sounds like it needs a little tuning. Mary-Kate really needs to work on playing the right notes, but the song turned out pretty good."

I breathed a big sigh of relief. Especially when we got a seven out of ten!

Backstage, Janelle hugged me. "We did it!"

"Xtreme rules!" I cheered.

I was so happy, I almost forgot that I'd had two guitar disasters in a row. But then I remembered the flying pick and the broken string. Diary, I think something is telling me that I should *not* be playing guitar!

Dear Diary,

Poor Mary-Kate. A busted string can happen to the biggest rock stars, but her heart just isn't in the guitar, or the sax, or the keyboard. She wants to sing!

Stringz was the next band up after Xtreme. Their version of "Greensleeves" got them a score of six.

Then it was time for Electric Pink!

163

I was so psyched when we climbed onto the stage. Erin plugged in her keyboard. Phoebe and I practiced a few chords. Phoebe was wearing a pale pink halter and capris, both of which used to be white – before the red sock got to them.

Phoebe mouthed, "Good luck."

I mouthed, "You too." I was pretty relieved that things seemed okay between us now.

"Electric Pink, do your stuff!" Stella announced.

We began to play "The Lonely Beach," and something awesome slowly happened: Everything seemed to gel. Erin's voice was stronger than ever. Phoebe and I jumped in with the chorus at just the right times.

As I played my guitar, I took a quick glance at the judges. Clarence and Sophie were swaying in their seats. Even Terrence was tapping his pencil against his cup.

"'What goes out always comes in with the tide,'" Erin sang. "'So, hey, baby, baby, don't run and hide!'"

When the song was over, we took our bows. The sound of everyone cheering gave me major goose bumps – the good kind!

"You're definitely high voltage, Electric Pink!" Clarence said. "Right on, girls, right on!"

"You proved to everyone that you're really in the pink," Sophie said. "And that's something to be proud of."

I gulped. What would Terrence have to say?

"I'm not going to lie," Terrence said. "You left the last stanza behind like some beached whale. . . . But not bad, Electric Pink . . . not bad at all."

Stella added up the judges' scores. "Electric Pink's in the lead with an eight!"

Backstage, we all jumped up and down. "Electric Pink is number one!" I cheered. "We even made Terrence smile!"

"Was my pink plan totally brilliant or what?" Erin asked. "It really helped our score!"

"So did my song," Phoebe pointed out.

"As soon as I added the 'hey, baby, baby's,'" Erin said. She picked up her keyboard and headed back to the seats.

"Did you hear what she said, Ashley?" Phoebe asked.

"I heard," I said. "But instead of fighting, the three of us should be celebrating a great score!"

"The *three* of us," Phoebe said. "Why does it always have to be the three of us? Why can't the *two* of us have fun together like we do in school?"

Phoebe had a point. We always did fun things together back in school. So why not in camp?

"Why don't we go kayaking on the lake?" I asked.

Phoebe smiled. "You mean the two of us?" she asked.

"Just you and me," I promised.

Chapter 9

Sunday

Dear Diary,

Atomic Pizza! That's our band's new name, as of last night. Janelle came up with it while we were eating pizza muffins for dinner.

Today we found out that the next round – the vocals round – is on Tuesday. Janelle and I will sing backup. Lark is still the lead vocalist.

After practice, the three of us stayed in the music room to talk about the next round. I stared down at my guitar. Bill fixed the broken string last night, but I didn't feel like playing it anymore. If only I could be as into an instrument as the rest of the kids were.

"Okay, Atomic Pizza," Janelle said. "What song should we sing in the next round?"

"How about the same song we sang in the last round?" Lark asked.

"Why don't we come up with something new?" I asked.

The three of us sat cross-legged on the floor and started brainstorming. It took us two hours, but we came up with lyrics to a song we called "Just Like You."

Lark tried singing it, but it didn't sound right. She couldn't get the beat.

"It's like this." I jumped up and pulled a pair of drumsticks off a shelf. I looked around for drums, but there weren't any in the room. So I picked up an aluminum wastebasket from the corner and tipped it over. Using the drumsticks, I began tapping out the beat.

"What do you think, Lark?" I asked. "Do you hear the rhythm now?"

Lark and Janelle were staring at me

"That is so metal, Mary-Kate," Janelle said.

"What is?" I asked, still tapping on the can. I was really getting into it.

"The way you're drumming," Janelle explained, "the sound totally rocks!"

"My mom once took me to a show called *Pulse*," Lark said. "The drummers were drumming on basins, buckets, cans – anything that made a noise. You sound just like them."

Basins? Buckets? Cans? Suddenly I had the best idea!

"Meet me outside our bunk," I said, slipping the drumsticks into my back pocket. "In about half an hour."

"Where are you going?" Janelle asked.

"No time to explain," I said as I raced out the door.

I ran all over camp collecting anything that I could make a beat on – buckets, basins, even an empty jumbo-size can of baked beans from the mess hall. I set them up in front of our bunk. Then I sat down on an upside-down bucket and found the rhythm.

Janelle and Lark hurried over.

"Go, Mary-Kate!" Lark cheered.

Soon, a group of instructors and campers came over to see what was going on. I didn't stop playing. I was having the best time trying out different sounds and beats.

"Play it, girl!" Ivy shouted.

For my big finish, I twirled the drumsticks between my fingers, then tossed them in the air. Everyone went wild, even though I only caught one drumstick. (I'll have to work on that, Diary.)

I saw Bill standing nearby.

"Hey, Bill. Can I drum on these buckets and basins for the next round?" I asked. "I promise I'll wash out the crusty cans so they don't smell like baked beans."

Bill shook his head. "Buckets, basins, and cans aren't exactly musical instruments, Mary-Kate," he said.

My heart sank. I'd finally found an instrument that fit me, and he wouldn't let me play it!

Stella stepped through the crowd and smiled. "Oh, Bill, lighten up!" she said. "Music is music, no matter how it's played."

Stella looked at me and said, "Try it out, Mary-Kate. And have fun with it."

"Ye-es!" I cheered. I took hold of both drumsticks and began to practice.

Diary, I know I'll never be a famous rock star playing buckets and basins. But, you know what? I'm having too much fun to care!

Dear Diary,

This morning on our break, Phoebe and I changed into swimsuits and went down to the lake. Buddy-time at last! Erin wasn't around, so I didn't feel bad about not including her. But when Phoebe and I reached the lake, all the kayaks and canoes were out on the water.

"Great," I said. "I really wanted to go kayaking. What do we do now?"

Phoebe kicked off her flip-flops. "Race you to the lake!" she called.

Phoebe and I charged into the water. We had tons of fun swimming and splashing each other. It was just like at school when we'd pal around for hours – just the two of us.

We swam back to shore and sat on our towels. I hugged my knees and gazed out at the lake. Phoebe lay on her back and stared up at the clouds. I could hear her singing something softly to herself. It sounded nice.

"What's that you're singing?" I asked.

"Just a song I've been making up in my head," Phoebe said. "You'll think it's corny."

"Try me," I urged.

"It's about the world coming together," Phoebe said. "But it's not finished yet."

"Then let's finish it," I said. "Maybe Electric Pink can sing it in the next round."

Phoebe grabbed her beach bag. She pulled out a pen and some stationery. Then we got to work writing lyrics.

In about an hour we wrote a whole song called "When the World Comes Together."

"Phoebe, I love it!" I exclaimed.

"Even though it has a message?" Phoebe said.

"It's a great message," I said. "What kid wouldn't want the world to come together?"

"What about Erin?" Phoebe asked. "What if she doesn't want to sing it?"

"We'll sing it, anyway," I declared.

We stood up and high-fived.

"Why didn't we think of this before?" I asked.

"You mean writing a song together?" Phoebe asked.

"Spending more time together!" I said.

Phoebe and I were about to roll up our towels when –

"Yo! Dudettes!"

We spun around. Erin was on the lake, waving from a bright red kayak. "Who wants to go kayaking?" she called.

"Are you finished with the kayak, Erin?" I asked.

"No," Erin called. "But I could sure use some company. Hop in, Ashley!"

I looked at the kayak Erin was using. It was a double kayak, designed for two people. With Erin inside, there was room for only one more.

"No, thanks," I called over the water. "There's not enough room for the three of us."

"Come on, Ashley. Just for a short ride," Erin called.

"Well . . ." I turned to Phoebe. "Would it be okay?"

"Go for it," Phoebe told me.

"Really?" I asked.

"You wanted to go kayaking," Phoebe said. "I guess I can find something else to do."

I looked at Phoebe, then at Erin. Phoebe didn't seem to mind, so . . .

"Ready or not, here I come!" I shouted.

The water splashed as I ran into the lake. Erin paddled the kayak into the shallow part, and I climbed in.

We paddled in perfect sync for a few minutes. Then Erin splashed me with her paddle and I splashed her back. Soon we were both splashing each other and laughing hysterically. I turned my head and saw Phoebe. She was still standing on the bank and she was frowning.

Is Phoebe angry? I wondered. *She can't be, can she?*

Erin and I had fun kayaking, but I couldn't stop wondering why Phoebe seemed so mad. Later I found her alone in our bunk, writing postcards.

"Phoebe, are you okay?" I asked.

"Do you care?" Phoebe said. She glared at me through her blue-frame glasses.

"Of course I care," I said. "What's going on?"

"I can't believe you did that, Ashley!"

"Did what?" I asked.

"You went kayaking with Erin," Phoebe said. "If you'd really wanted to hang with me, you would have told her no!"

Did I have water in my ears? Was I hearing right?

Was Phoebe mad at me for doing something she had told me to do?

"Phoebe, you said it was okay for me to go kayaking," I reminded her. "You said you'd do something else."

"I only said that because I wanted to see what you would do," Phoebe said.

"What?" I cried. "You mean it was – a test?"

Phoebe didn't answer.

I heard some loud banging behind the bunk. Through the back window I saw Mary-Kate drumming on a bunch of cans. *Is there a full moon or something?* I wondered.

"Meet my new set of drums!" Mary-Kate said as I went outside. "Stella said I can play them in the next round!"

"And after the round you can recycle them," I joked. But I didn't feel much like laughing.

I sat down on the grass next to Mary-Kate and told her the latest. "Why is Phoebe being so unfair?" I asked.

"I guess it's hard to be fair when you think your best friend is slipping away," Mary-Kate said.

"But I'm not." I shook my head. "I don't get it."

"Think about it," Mary-Kate said. "Phoebe doesn't like you spending so much time with Erin."

"So what am I supposed to do?" I asked. "Choose only one friend?"

"No," Mary-Kate said. "You have to find some way for Erin and Phoebe to be friends so you can *all* be friends!"

"I know." I sighed. "But it's not that easy!"

Any bright ideas, Diary?

Chapter 10

Monday

Dear Diary,

Crush! That's our band's new name, starting today. Janelle came up with that one when she confessed she has a crush on a roadie named Hank. And guess what else happened today? Just as Crush was about to practise, Stella walked into our music room with a huge surprise. . . .

"You got another care package, Lark," Stella said. She smiled so wide, I could see her gums. "It's from your dad!"

Lark's mouth tightened into a thin line. "Oh . . . terrific," she said.

The package was from London again. It was smaller than the last one. I was dying to know what was inside. "Aren't you going to open it, Lark?" Stella asked.

"Yeah, aren't you curious?" Bill added.

Lark shrugged. "I'll open it when I get back to my bunk," she replied. "It's probably no big deal."

"Hey, *anything* from Rodney Beecham is a big deal!" Bill exclaimed. "He's the big cheese of rock!"

"Open it now!" Stella pleaded. "Go ahead!"

Lark sucked in her breath as she tore open the package. "It's sheet music," she said. "And a tape."

There was a note inside too. Lark's face dropped as she read it. "Um . . . my dad wrote a song for our band," she told us. "He wants us to sing it in the next round."

"Yes!" Bill cheered. "My band is going to sing a Rodney Beecham original! How cool is that?"

Janelle and I exchanged grins. We were pretty stoked about singing a Rodney Beecham song, too.

"Sorry," Lark said, quietly packing everything back into the box. "I'm not doing it."

"Why not?" Stella and Bill asked at the same time.

"The song was probably his manager's idea," Lark said. "Just like sending me to this camp. My dad is probably going along with it because it'll make him look good."

The room got quiet. The Corral Chicks and some girls from Stringz were standing at the door, listening in.

Stella put her arm around Lark. "Singing a Rodney Beecham song would be great for Camp Rock 'n' Roll," she said. "We could write about it in our next brochure. Maybe we could even make it the camp anthem."

Lark looked totally embarrassed and miserable.

"Why don't you just try out the song?" Bill suggested. "If you don't like it, we can ditch it."

Lark looked at me. "What do you think, Mary-Kate?"

"Can't hurt to see what it sounds like," I said.

Lark still didn't look sure. But she folded the note and said, "Okay. Let's give it a shot."

Stella and Bill checked out the sheet music. I could hear the girls at the door mumbling.

"Too bad my dad isn't a famous rock star," said a Corral Chick. "Then my band would come in first place."

This must be Lark's worst nightmare, I thought. I walked over to the open door. "This is a private practise," I said, then I shut the door hard.

Janelle and I went over to Lark. She was staring at the sheet music, shaking her head. "And just how does he expect us to learn a whole new song by tomorrow?"

"We'll practise together until we do," Janelle said.

"We're not just a band – we're a team!" I said. "Like your football team back home."

Lark's face lit up when I said the word "football." For her, it was the magic word!

"Okay," Bill said. "Let's see if we can play this."

Camp Rock 'n' Roll

From the first time we played the song, it sounded great. Lark didn't look happy, but her voice soared.

Wait till her dad sees her perform, I thought. *He'll be so proud!*

Dear Diary,

Today we really got off on the wrong foot. I say "foot" because when we woke up this morning, all of our trainers were missing!

"It's a trainers raid!" Janelle said as we inspected our messed-up cubbies. "Every summer one of the bunks sneaks into the other bunks to steal everyone's trainers."

"What do they do with them?" Mary-Kate asked her.

Janelle pointed out the window. We ran to it and looked outside. Dangling from the branches of a big oak tree were dozens of trainers – all sizes, shapes, and colors!

"Which bunk did this?" Phoebe asked.

Suddenly a song blared from the loudspeaker. It was "Material Girl."

"Bunk Madonna!" we said at the same time.

Sure enough, out by the tree, Bunk Madonna was high-fiving. And above them, dangling from one of the oak's highest branches, were my blue and yellow trainers.

"Okay, Bunk Elvis," Mary-Kate said. "Let's show Bunk Madonna they can't mess with our blue suede shoes!" Things got goofy as we climbed the tree to get our trainers back. Everyone was giggling and having a good time – until Erin climbed down holding a plaid trainer.

"Phoebe, this must be yours," Erin said, holding it out. "It looks like it's from the nineteen fifties."

"Really?" Phoebe said. She lifted a berry-colored trainers off the ground. "This must be yours. It's pink!"

Erin smiled and said, "I don't have pink sneakers. But if I did, they'd be *new*."

"You have no idea what real fashion is," Phoebe said. "You just wear the stuff your mom gives you from her magazine."

"Just because your clothes are old doesn't make them cool," Erin shot back.

I groaned, not sure how to stop their fighting. It was lucky the bell for breakfast rang.

All during breakfast I was dreading band practise. I still hadn't shown Erin the song that Phoebe and I had written.

What if Erin hates the song? I wondered. *Will Phoebe blame me if Erin refuses to sing it?*

But during band practice something amazing happened. Erin liked the song!

"The message is nice," Erin said. "And I can do some cool things on the keyboard to really make it rock." She went over to her keyboard and started to play.

Phoebe watched her from the corner of her eye. "I don't trust her, Ashley," she whispered. "How come Erin suddenly likes something I wrote? She never did before."

"I'm not taking sides, Phoebe," I said very carefully. "But try giving Erin a chance. Okay?"

Phoebe twanged a guitar string. "I'll try."

"Thanks," I said. I didn't have a clue why things were suddenly working. Maybe Erin saw that she was coming between Phoebe and me, so she decided to be extra nice. Or maybe she just liked our song.

And maybe, just maybe, I thought, *this song will help Erin and Phoebe finally hit it off and be friends!*

Chapter 11

Tuesday

Dear Diary,

Guess who came to Camp Rock 'n' Roll today? Come on, guess. Here's a hint: He came in a stretch limo, and he wore a black leather jacket and wraparound shades.

Yup – it was Rodney Beecham, rock superstar and Lark's dad!

Rodney's limo pulled into camp this morning while we were getting ready for round number two. When word got out that he was here, everyone ran to see him.

Like most celebs, Rodney wasn't alone. He came with his manager, Doris, and press agent, Lou. There were a bunch of other people, but I had no idea what they were supposed to be doing. Lou snapped a slew of pictures as Stella ran to greet Rodney.

"Stella Vickers!" Rodney shouted. He pointed to her and said, "You built this camp on rock 'n' roll, girl!"

Though I couldn't admit it to Lark, I was excited, too. Having a real rock superstar in our camp was awesome!

Rodney signed a bunch of autographs. I wanted one, but I didn't want to act like another fan in front of Lark.

When Rodney was finished with the autographs he walked over to Lark. "How's my girl?" he asked with a thick British accent. "Singing like a little lark, no doubt!"

"Hi, Dad," Lark said.

"What brings you to camp, Rod?" Stella asked. "We didn't expect you until the taping of the special."

Doris answered. "Mr. Beecham has come to hear his daughter sing with Atomic Burger," she said.

"It was Atomic *Pizza*," Lark mumbled. "Now we're Crush."

"Suuu-per!" Rodney exclaimed.

"Mr. Beecham also wants to hear the song he wrote especially for her," Doris went on.

"And to make sure she's ready for the TV special," Rodney added. "We're calling it *Getting Mod with Rod*!"

Lark's mouth became a thin grim line.

"You picked the perfect time, Rodney," Stella said. "The girls are competing in the vocals round today."

"Vocals? As in singing?" Rodney shouted happily. "Fantastic!"

Stella put her arm around Rodney's shoulders. "There's coffee and doughnuts in the lounge, Rodney," she said.

"Suuuuu-per!" Rodney shouted again.

Most of the kids followed Rodney and his crew to the lounge. I stayed behind with Lark.

"I wish he'd told me he was coming today," Lark said. She started biting her nails. I kind of understood why she looked so nervous. Not only did the judges have to like her singing today – so did her dad.

"Everything will be great, Lark," I said. "We're a team, remember?"

"Yeah, a team," Lark said and tried to smile.

Later, when Crush walked into the theatre, Rodney was there, sitting with the judges.

Janelle interrupted my thoughts. "How do you like my new hair colour?" she asked. She whipped off her hat, revealing neon purple streaks. "It's called Grape Expectations. You can use it for the next round."

"Nope," I said, shaking my head.

"Not even the tips?" Janelle asked.

Janelle, Lark, and I took our usual seats in the theater. I glanced back at Ashley. She was sitting between Erin and Phoebe. All three of them were smiling and talking to one another.

A good sign, I thought.

Stella walked to the microphone and welcomed everyone. Then she introduced Rodney. The campers went wild again as he stood up and waved.

I looked at Lark from the corner of my eye. Her hands were shaking in her lap.

I guess I'd be nervous, too, if I was singing for my dad, I thought. *And my dad isn't even a famous rock star.*

The round started with The Corral Chicks. This time they'd gotten rid of the washboard for a harpsichord.

Somewhere in the middle of their song, Rodney jumped onstage. He snatched one of the girl's Western hats and plopped it on his head. Then he began dancing a fancy two-step across the stage!

The audience loved it. They especially loved it when Rodney goofed with the judges, leading everyone in boos when Terrence gave his score.

"Your dad's a riot!" Janelle whispered to Lark.

Lark didn't answer. She stared straight ahead and squeezed the arms of her chair.

"Now we'll hear from Crush!" Stella announced.

"Go for it!" Bill whispered from the row behind us.

I gripped my drumsticks as we marched onto the stage. I set up my buckets and cans. Janelle plugged her guitar into an amp. Lark stood behind the mike.

The roadies left the stage, and the theater became quiet. Janelle played the first set of chords, and Crush began to perform.

Janelle and I started the song with the backing vocals. Then Lark came in with the lead. But as I kept the beat on my buckets, something didn't sound right. It was Lark's voice. It was shaky and off-key.

I glanced into the audience at Rodney. He had a pained look on his face as he listened to Lark.

Uh-oh, I thought. *He hates the way Lark is singing.*

I decided to do something – anything – to take Rodney's attention away from Lark. I twirled my drumsticks and tossed them up in the air. I made funny faces. I even wore one of the rubber pails on my head!

I must have looked totally outrageous, but it worked. Rodney wasn't watching Lark anymore. He was watching me.

When our song was over, Terrence spoke first. "Lark, you need to work on your delivery." He looked at me and smirked. "And Mary-Kate, try not to deliver so much!"

We got a score of seven, which was pretty good. Bill gave us a thumbs-up sign as we carried our instruments backstage. As I was stacking my gear in a corner I heard a voice say, "Well done, Mary-Kate!"

The accent was definitely British. And the only person around with a British accent was –

"Rodney Beecham!" I gasped as I spun around.

Rodney stood behind me with a big grin. "You've got it rockin' on, love," he said. "Keep up the good work!"

My mouth hung open as Rodney walked away. It stayed that way practically all day long!

Diary, I knew I liked to play the buckets and cans. But I never dreamed I'd get a thumbs-up from a famous rock star like Rodney Beecham. This had to be my *best* day ever!

Dear Diary,

This had to be my *worst* day ever!

It started out pretty well. Erin and Phoebe sat next to each other at breakfast and at lunch. Erin even gave Phoebe the tomato slices from her tuna sandwich.

"I can't believe the vocals round is today," Phoebe said. "Does everyone know the words to our song?"

Erin nodded. "Like the back of my hand."

Phoebe was dressed in pink from head to toe. She had borrowed a pink miniskirt, blouse, and shoes from the costume cabin last night. Even her lip gloss was pink!

I felt all warm and fuzzy inside. Everyone was getting along at last!

The three of us sat together in the theatre, too. We all had fun watching Rodney Beecham and the other bands. Crush rocked, thanks to Mary-Kate. She was out of control on the buckets and cans. Then Gemini sang about a planet ruled by girls. A band called Knee Jerk sang about breaking up with a boyfriend.

After that, it was time for Electric Pink!

"Remember, guys," Jennifer whispered as we stood in the wings, "do your best, but don't forget to have fun!"

My heart raced as we ran onstage. Erin sat at her keyboard. Phoebe and I stood with our guitars.

"Blimey!" Rodney Beecham said, slipping on his black sunglasses. "I think I have pinkeye!"

Erin played the first few notes. Then she began to sing. I blinked. The words were totally *different*. The song wasn't about the world getting together – it was about Erin and some cute guy getting together!

What's she doing? I wondered in a panic. *I can't believe she changed the words!*

I glanced at Phoebe. She was singing through gritted teeth. We stuck to our original words as we sang backup.

Erin did *not*!

"'Don't forget, baby, I'll be waiting after school,'" Erin sang. "'When our hands come together, it will be so cool!'"

"'World come together, world come together,'" Phoebe and I sang. "'World come together – ooooh!'"

I was so glad when the song was over! Phoebe and I stared at Erin. She just smiled and gave us a little shrug.

"Thanks, Electric Pink," Stella said. She turned to the judges. "What was your take on that number, guys?"

I held my breath. I expected Terrence to totally trash us. Instead, he said, "Interesting. I never heard a song that compared a junior high school crush to world peace before."

"Deep, man," Rodney said, nodding. "Real deep."

I couldn't believe it when Electric Pink scored a nine. It was the highest score in the round so far!

Jennifer jumped up from her seat and cheered.

Backstage, Erin and I jumped up and down, too. Not Phoebe. She stood with her hands folded across her chest.

"Okay, Erin," Phoebe said. "What was that all about?"

"What do you mean?" Erin asked.

"As if you don't know," Phoebe said. "You changed the words of our song without telling us!"

"Oh, that," Erin said. "I decided to tweak the words last night after everybody was asleep. I was going to tell you today, but when Rodney showed up, things got so crazy."

"He arrived this morning," Phoebe pointed out. "You had plenty of time to tell us!"

"What's the big deal?" Erin asked. Her blue eyes sparkled. "We got an awesome score, didn't we?"

"Don't just stand there, Ashley," Phoebe said. "Why don't you say something?"

What could I say but the truth?

"You really should have told us about the new words, Erin," I said. "Band members have to be on the same page."

"You see?" Phoebe said to Erin.

Then I looked at Phoebe and said, "But we did end up getting a fabulous score. So why don't we forget about it?"

"Are you telling me to forget it?" Phoebe asked.

"I said *we* should forget it."

"You meant me," Phoebe said.

Erin shook her head. She picked up her keyboard and walked back to her seat. I turned to Phoebe.

"Come on, Phoebe. Maybe you don't think it's right that Erin changed our song. And I understand that. But you've got to admit it turned out great."

Phoebe's shoulders dropped. "Don't you get it, Ashley?" she asked. "Don't you see that you totally broke your promise? You said back at school that we'd always st – "

"Ashley!" a voice cut in.

I spun around. Mary-Kate was running toward me.

"You did it, you did it!" Mary-Kate cried. "My sister got a nine score!"

"Do you believe it?" I squealed. "We just started playing and everything clicked!"

Mary-Kate and I hugged. From the corner of my eye I saw Phoebe. She was walking away with her guitar. I let go of Mary-Kate.

"Ashley?" Mary-Kate said. "What's wrong with Phoebe? She looks kind of upset."

"Phoebe's bummed out that Erin changed the words to our song," I said. "But I'm sure she'll get over it once it hits her what a great score we got."

"You're probably right," Mary-Kate said.

"Well . . . maybe I should go talk to Phoebe," I said. I turned to follow her.

"Later," Mary-Kate said as Venus took their places onstage. She grabbed my hand. "We'd better get back to our seats now."

By the time the round was over, Electric Pink was tied with Venus in overall score. Everyone headed to the rec hall for a huge pizza party. I thought I'd find Phoebe there, but I didn't.

"Doesn't this remind you of the pizza parties at school, Ashley?" Mary-Kate asked as she grabbed a slice.

I looked around the rec hall. Rodney and the instructors were jamming on their instruments while we ate five different types of pizza.

"Just the pizza part," I said. "We never had a famous rock star at school."

There was something else that was different: Phoebe wasn't there. At the White Oak pizza parties, we'd rip our slices in half so we could share toppings. We'd even eat our slices the same way by tearing off the gooey cheese first.

I glanced over at Erin. She was eating her pizza with a knife and fork. Bor-ring!

All of a sudden, I really missed Phoebe, Diary. I couldn't stop thinking about her.

"You know, Mary-Kate," I said. "Maybe I have been siding too much with Erin."

Mary-Kate's mouth was full with pizza. All she could say was, "Mmmph?"

"Maybe I was more wowed by Erin's clothes and her coolness than I thought," I went on. "And I kind of did break my promise to stick together with Phoebe."

"Mm-mmph."

"There's only one thing to do," I said with a nod. "I'm going to find Phoebe and apologise to her right now!"

Mary-Kate finally swallowed. "Go for it," she said.

I went straight to our bunk. "Are you here, Phoebe?" I called as I stepped inside.

The bunk wasn't dark yet. I could see Phoebe lying on the top bed, wrapped in her comforter. Her eyes were closed as if she was asleep – or pretending to be.

"Phoebe?" I tried again. She still didn't answer. Maybe she really was asleep.

I put the pizza down and gently nudged her shoulder. "Phoebe, it's me. I really need to talk to you."

"Mmmm," Phoebe murmured in her sleep. Then she rolled over.

"But Phoebe . . ." I tried again.

Phoebe didn't answer. I guess she really was asleep.

There's plenty of time, I told myself. *I'll straighten things out with Phoebe first thing tomorrow morning.*

And from now on, Diary, Phoebe Cahill is going to come first.

Chapter 12

Wednesday

Dear Diary,

Help! The first thing I wanted to do this morning was apologise to Phoebe. I climbed out of my bottom bunk.

"Hey, Phoebe," I started to stay. "I want to talk . . ."

I never even finished my sentence. Phoebe's paisley throws were gone. So were her sheets and comforter. Worst of all – Phoebe was gone!

"Everyone, wake up!" I shouted. "Phoebe is missing!"

Mary-Kate opened one eye. "Phoebe's cubby is empty, too," she pointed out.

Ivy came into the bunk, yawning.

"Ivy," I said, "where's Phoebe?"

"Phoebe called her mom and dad last night. She told them she didn't want to stay at camp."

My blood froze. "She . . . what?"

"They had Phoebe's Aunt Marie, who lives in Philadelphia, pick her up this morning," Ivy went on. She yawned again. "Very early this morning."

"What's going to happen to our band?" Erin asked.

I glared at Erin. Was that all she could think about?

While the others washed up, I sat on my bed. Mary-Kate sat next to me. "I don't get it," I said. "If Phoebe hated it here so much, why didn't she talk to me about it?"

"I don't know, Ashley," Mary-Kate said. "But you said you knew she was upset."

"I had no idea she was upset enough to leave!" I said. "She didn't try hard enough to let me know."

"Maybe she thought she shouldn't have to try so hard to get her best friend's attention," Mary-Kate said quietly.

I stared at my twin as she stood up and walked to her cubby. Had I been that bad a best friend?

I had to find Phoebe and talk to her fast. I quickly washed, dressed, and raced to the main office.

"Please," I begged Gloria, the camp secretary, "I have to know where Phoebe Cahill went so I can call her."

"Phoebe's new phone number is confidential," Gloria said. "It can only be given out in an emergency."

"This *is* an emergency," I said. "Our friendship is on the line!"

"Sorry," Gloria said. "Maybe she'll call you later."

I ran around the camp asking everyone where Phoebe had gone. Jennifer didn't know. Stella said the same thing Gloria did: Phoebe's phone number in Philly was top secret.

Diary, I couldn't think about music all day. Or the next choreography round. All I could think was: Did I drive my best friend away?

Dear Diary,

I've got bad news . . . and totally awesome, heel-clicking, heart-stopping, amazing news.

First, the bad news: Phoebe left camp, and Ashley feels awful. I feel awful, too. I really like Phoebe and was glad she'd come to Camp Rock 'n' Roll.

Now the good news: Right before our dance workshop, Janelle, Lark, and I were by the lake, talking.

"I'm worried about this next round," Janelle said. "I can't chew gum and play my guitar at the same time. How am I going to play my guitar and *dance* at the same time?"

"Elvis did it." I grabbed Janelle's guitar and sang as I shook my knees. "'A hunk, a hunk of burning love – '"

"Bravo!" a voice interrupted. It was Rodney's voice!

Great, I thought, turning slowly. *I just made a total jerk of myself in front of Rodney Beecham!*

Rodney was walking toward the lake. His manager and press agent were hurrying behind him.

"You're just the girl I want to see, Mary-Jane!" Rodney said as they got closer.

"Um . . . it's Mary-Kate," I said. "But you can call me Mary-Jane if you'd like."

"Super!" Rodney laughed. He turned to his crew. "You see? I told you she was funny."

Lou and Doris laughed along. Lark didn't.

Rodney pointed his finger at me and said, "How would *you* like to perform with *me* on my TV special?"

My eyes popped wide open. *Rodney Beecham, international superstar, wants to perform with me? Me?*

"I . . . I . . . I don't get it," I stammered. "What about Lark? Isn't she supposed to sing with you?"

"Lark isn't comfortable singing in public," Rodney explained. "I saw that yesterday during the round."

Lark's eyes looked hurt. But she smiled and said, "It's okay, Mary-Kate, he told me this already. I'm cool with it."

"You're a natural performer, Mary-Kate," Rodney said. "I'd like you to play your buckets while I sing.

You can sing backup, too. I'm writing the song now," he added. "It's called 'Lively Girl.'"

By now my head was spinning. Was I that Lively Girl? Was Rodney writing a song just for me?

"Rodney is catching a plane to London in two hours," Doris said. "He needs your answer ASAP."

I opened my mouth to speak but didn't know what to say. No one had ever asked me to perform on television before.

"Do it, Mary-Kate," Janelle whispered. "You may never get this chance again."

I pictured myself singing with Rodney Beecham on national TV. I pictured all my friends watching.

"Yes!" I blurted out. "The answer is yes!"

"Suuuu-per!" Rodney exclaimed.

"I have to call my dad for permission," I said.

"He'll have to sign a release form, too," Doris said. "That gives *us* permission to show you on TV."

"I'm sure your dad will approve," Rodney said. "What father wouldn't want to see his daughter perform on TV?"

I saw Lark lower her eyes.

"We'll come back the last week of camp for the final round," the manager said. "And to tape the special."

"Then we'll roooock!" Rodney said.

Lou snapped a picture of me. Rodney gave Lark a hug. Then they and Doris hurried up the hill to the waiting limo.

"Thank you!" I called after them. I turned to Janelle and Lark and squealed, "I can't belieeeeve it! Ohmigosh! I have to tell Ashley!"

Chapter 13

Thursday

Dear Diary,

Since yesterday I've had Phoebe on the brain. I can't stop thinking about how to reach her!

I tried calling Phoebe's mom and dad in San Francisco, but I kept getting their answering machine.

Are they on their way to Philadelphia to bring Phoebe home? I wondered. *I hope not!*

I tried e-mailing Phoebe from the camp office, but she never e-mailed me back.

"It's all my fault," I told Mary-Kate at breakfast. "I never should have put Erin before Phoebe!"

Mary-Kate stared at me, starry-eyed. "I can't believe it, Ashley," she said. "I'm going to sing on TV. Me!"

I smiled at my sister. Her head was still in the clouds and that was okay. I am happy for her. But unhappy for Phoebe – and me.

Band practice later just made it worse. . . .

"Now that Phoebe left," Jennifer told Erin and me, "the two of you will have to perform as a duo."

"A duo?" I repeated. It sounded so final. As though Phoebe wasn't coming back!

"That's so cool." Erin squealed. "Just you and me – right, Ashley? Maybe we can wear the exact same outfits! And call ourselves Electric Pink Times 2!"

I whirled to face Erin. "It's not cool," I told her. "Phoebe is my best friend!"

Maybe I did overreact, Diary. But at that moment I also made up my mind.

I'm going to find Phoebe and get her to come back to Camp Rock 'n' Roll. No matter what it takes!

Dear Diary,

Just when I thought everything was perfect, I found out something that really reeked!

At the end of the day my bunk mates decided to celebrate my good news. So instead of going to the mess hall for dinner, Ivy ordered two pizzas. We brought in a boom box and blasted all kinds of music – rap, rock, even a few oldies from the fifties. Hey, this is Bunk Elvis!

But Ashley wasn't in the mood to celebrate with us. She was still hurting over Phoebe. Lark was acting gloomy, too. She had been like that ever since her dad left. After we finished the pizza, Janelle made a toast with a can of orange soda. "To Mary-Kate, the future Queen of Rock!" she declared. "May she remember us when she's at the top . . . and when we all want tickets to major rock concerts!"

Everyone clapped and whistled. Only Lark didn't join in. She stood up, excused herself, and left the bunk.

"Is it something I said?" Janelle asked.

"Probably not," I said, standing up. "I'll find out what's bothering her."

I left Bunk Elvis to look for Lark. She was exactly where I thought I'd find her: on the playing field, bouncing a football on one knee.

"Shoot it here!" I called.

Lark kicked the ball over to me, and I kicked it back. We didn't say a word as we kicked the ball back and forth. Finally I had to speak up.

"What's up, Lark?" I asked. "You've been acting kind of weird ever since your dad left yesterday."

Lark put her foot on top of the ball to keep it from rolling. I could see her chin quivering.

"I *don't* like singing in public," she said. "But I still wanted my dad to be proud of me. That's why I was so nervous in the vocals round."

"I figured that," I said, nodding.

"Then he asked you to be in the TV special instead of me," Lark said. "He made me feel like such a loser."

"But," I said slowly, "when your dad asked me, you said it was okay."

"What else could I say?" Lark asked. "My dad has no idea how bad he made me feel."

I'd had no idea how Lark really felt, either. And it made me feel horrible!

"Listen, I won't do the special," I told her. "You're a much better singer than I am, anyway."

Lark shook her head. "You're the better performer," she said. "And that's what Dad wants."

"How can I do the special?" I asked. "Look how upset you are!"

"I'll deal with it." Lark looked me straight in the eye. "Just promise me you'll do the special, Mary-Kate."

I noticed the studded bracelet around Lark's wrist. It was the friendship bracelet I had given her in arts and crafts.

How could I do this to my new friend? How could I come between her and her dad?

"No way, Lark," I said, shaking my head.

"Do it, Mary-Kate," Lark insisted. "If you don't, my dad will know how upset I am. He'll think I'm a big baby."

Lark wasn't crying anymore. The look on her face told me she was serious. "If you're my friend," she said, "you'll promise me."

"Okay," I said slowly. "I promise."

"Good." Lark sniffed. She wiped her face with the sleeve of her red hoodie. "We'd better get back to the bunk before they come looking for us."

"Yeah," I said, forcing a smile.

We left the ball on the field and headed back to Bunk Elvis. Lark started chatting about her favorite soccer players. I hardly heard her, because all I could think about was the TV special.

It's not right, I thought. *Rodney Beecham shouldn't be performing with me – he should be performing with his daughter. He should be performing with Lark!*

I gazed at the sun going down behind the trees.

Then again, I thought, *this is my chance to be on TV with a rock superstar!*

Diary, what would you do if you were me?

Would you pick friendship?

Or *fame*?

mary-kateandashley
TWO of a kind™
Diaries

Twist and Shout

by Judy Katschke

HarperCollins_Entertainment_
An Imprint of HarperCollinsPublishers

A PARACHUTE PRESS BOOK

Chapter 1

Thursday

Dear Diary,

I'm so psyched! Ashley and I have been at Camp Rock 'n' Roll for two whole weeks. And here's the best part: We have *two whole weeks* left to go.

Camp Rock 'n' Roll is an all-girls camp in Pennsylvania. We're here to learn all about putting together a rock band. I've already made really cool friends – friends like Lark Maitland. Lark and I share all kinds of things: Bunk Elvis, for instance (all the bunks are named after rock stars) – and a serious love of football!

Today, before we headed over to the camp barbecue, Lark and I worked up an appetite on the football Pitch. She has an awesome kick.

"Wow," I said as I watched her ball disappear over the trees.

"Where do you think it landed?" Lark asked, shading her brown eyes with her hand.

"Probably on the barbecue grill," I said. "I think I just heard a sizzle."

"Omigosh! The barbecue!" Lark exclaimed. "What if they already ran out of watermelon?"

"That would be the *worst*," I joked.

We ran to the barbecue so fast, Lark's long dark hair bounced on her shoulders. Halfway there, she stopped. "I almost forgot," she said. "I have something for you."

She held up her arm to show me the studded leather bracelet I'd given her. "You made me a friendship bracelet in arts and crafts," she said. "So I made you one, too!" She reached into the pocket of her jeans, then dropped a bracelet with silver and turquoise beads into my hand.

"It's awesome!" I said. I slipped the bracelet on my wrist. "Thanks, Lark."

It's still hard to believe that Lark and I are friends. I've never known anyone who was rock royalty before. Lark's dad, Rodney Beecham, is a world-famous rock star with a huge mansion in England and a gazillion platinum records. But Lark is totally down-to-earth. We have tons of stuff in common. We both love sports, soggy cornflakes, and wearing sneakers all the time.

At the barbecue, Lark and I joined my sister, Ashley, and our other bunk mate, Janelle Chow, on the grass. Janelle's spiky black hair was stuffed into a backward baseball cap. She looked totally metal in her black shirt and studded bracelets. The only thing missing was her electric guitar.

Twist and Shout

"Hamburger," Janelle mumbled as she stared at her paper plate. "Hot dog . . . root beer . . . coleslaw . . ."

I stared at Janelle. Why was she acting so weird?

"Potato salad," Janelle kept mumbling. "Lemonade . . . barbecue sauce . . ."

"Janelle, what are you doing?" I finally asked.

"I was just thinking up more names for our band," Janelle said. "How about the Dill Pickles?"

Everyone at Camp Rock 'n' Roll is in a three-girl band. Lark sings and plays tambourine. Ashley and Janelle play electric guitar. I play a mean set of drums – well, more like four jumbo tin cans, three upside-down pails, and two aluminum buckets. My drums may look funky, but once I get the beat – watch out!

Janelle, Lark, and I are in a band we've been calling Crush. But before that it was The Diva Dollz, Xtreme – even Atomic Pizza!

"You guys change your band name more than most people change their socks!" Ashley joked.

"Let's stick with Crush, Janelle," I said. "'The Dill Pickles' sounds like some cartoon show."

"Fine with me," Janelle said. She picked up some corn on the cob. "Now I can concentrate on the Battle of the Bands!"

The Battle of the Bands is the highlight of camp. The contest includes four different categories:

harmony, vocals, choreography, and songwriting. The bands with the highest scores in the preliminary rounds compete for title of Best Band. So far, Ashley's band, Electric Pink, is tied with a band called Venus.

Even though her band was tied for first place, Ashley was too upset to be very happy about it. Her best friend, Phoebe Cahill, had just left camp, and I knew my sister blamed herself. Phoebe and Ashley were practically super-glued together at the White Oak Academy for Girls, our boarding school. But things didn't work out so well here at Camp Rock 'n' Roll.

"I'm getting seconds," Lark announced. "This potato salad is just too good." She stood up and strolled to the picnic tables.

"So, are you getting nervous about being in the music special?" Janelle asked me.

It's true, Diary! Lark's dad, Rodney Beecham, asked me to be in his TV special!

Sounds great, right? Just one problem: Lark was supposed to appear in that special with her dad. So now I feel weird that he picked me instead.

"I'm going to tell you something," I said in a low voice. "But don't repeat it to anyone else!"

"What?" Janelle said. She and Ashley leaned in close.

212

"I don't think I'm going to do the special," I said.

Janelle stared at me. "Have you been drinking too much fruit juice, Mary-Kate?" she said. "How can you *not* do the special?"

"Because Lark should be in it," I said. "Not me."

"But Rodney said she wasn't ready," Ashley said. "Her stage fright in the vocals round was too bad."

"Lark is really upset about that," I said. I told them more about Lark. How her parents are divorced. And the only time she sees her famous dad is when he plays a concert near her home in Santa Fe, New Mexico.

"Did Lark tell you she doesn't want you to do the special?" Janelle asked.

"No," I said. "She even made me promise not to drop out. She doesn't want her dad to know how hurt she really feels."

"How do *you* feel about it?" Ashley asked me.

I frowned. "Of course, part of me really wants to do it. It's a once-in-a-lifetime opportunity. I mean, being on TV with Rodney Beecham would be awesome! The other part knows that Lark should be performing with her dad, not me."

I reached up to brush my strawberry-blonde hair out of my face and noticed the friendship bracelet

Lark gave me. The bracelet decided it: My friendship with Lark should come first. "I'm calling Rodney Beecham tomorrow," I declared. "To tell him I'm *not* doing the TV special."

Dear Diary,

I think I'm the only one at camp who *didn't* have fun at the barbecue. I tried, Diary, I really tried, but I couldn't stop thinking about Phoebe.

Phoebe Cahill isn't just my roommate at school – she's my best friend. That's why I begged Phoebe to come to Camp Rock 'n' Roll with me. I even promised her that I'd always stick with her at camp no matter what.

But that was *before* I met Erin Verko. Erin is our bunkmate and she's totally hip. Her mom is the editor of *Teen Scene* magazine, so Erin came to camp with a rack full of cutting-edge clothes. (And Diary, you know how much I love clothes!) She's also really fun to hang out with.

I thought Erin was the best thing since quick-dry nail polish. I agreed with everything she wanted for our band, Electric Pink. I even started spending more time with Erin than Phoebe.

Phoebe tried to tell me how she felt, but I guess I

wasn't listening. So Phoebe and I had a big fight, and then she left camp before dawn. Just like that!

Diary, I know I broke my promise to Phoebe. And I want to apologise, I really do – but I can't find her. All I know is that Phoebe is staying with her aunt in Philadelphia. The camp office won't give me her address or telephone number because it's "private information."

Without Phoebe, things aren't the same – especially with the band. I really missed her at music practice. Phoebe and I used to play our guitars side by side. She played lead. I played rhythm. It's hard to play rhythm by yourself! But music practice continued today – even though Electric Pink is now a duo instead of a trio.

"Since you're tied with Venus for first place, that'll be the band to beat," Jennifer said. Her long curly black hair hung over her shoulders. She wore her black GUITAR GODDESS T-shirt, jeans, and lots of chunky silver jewellery. "The focus of the next round is on choreography."

"Does that mean we have to outdance Venus?" I asked.

"Choreography isn't just about dancing," Jennifer said. "It's about presentation, so costumes and special effects count, too."

Jennifer showed us some famous rock videos. My favorite was one from the eighties called "Walk Like an Egyptian." Not only did the girls wear fancy Egyptian costumes, they came up with their own dance, too!

"Now, what will your band do?" Jennifer asked us.

Erin jumped up from her chair. She was wearing red cargo shorts with a matching halter top. I recognised the outfit right away from the July issue of *Teen Scene*.

"I say we put down our instruments in the middle of the song," she said. "Then we shake it up like this!" Erin swung her arms and shook her hips. Her long blond hair whipped back and forth as she started to sing, "'When the world gets together, yeah, yeah, yeeeeeah!'"

It's a good thing Phoebe isn't here, I thought. *This is just the type of dancing she hates!*

"What do you think, Ashley?" Erin asked when she stopped. "I want you to be totally honest."

Honest? I took a deep breath, then said, "All that shaking is more like aerobics than dancing. In fact, just watching you made my teeth rattle. You reminded me of a bobble-head doll. In a speeding car."

"I didn't mean *that*, honest!" Erin said, her eyes wide with surprise.

Of course she's surprised, I realised. I had never disagreed with her before.

"Sorry, Erin," I said. "I didn't mean to hurt your feelings."

"It's okay," Erin said. "But for a minute there, you sounded like Phoebe."

Phoebe. She never agreed with any of Erin's ideas. But just hearing her name made me miss her all over again.

Suddenly I knew exactly what I had to do.

Somehow I'm going to find Phoebe. And then I'm going to get her to come back to camp!

Chapter 2

Friday

Dear Diary,

Today our band, Crush, had our first dance practice in the music building.

"We can't come up with a dance number until we pick a song to sing," I said, twirling my drumsticks in my hands.

Our instructor, Bill, leaned back in his chair. He was wearing one of his Led Zeppelin tees and ripped-up jeans.

"You know, you *can* sing the same song you sang in the last round," Bill told us.

"You mean the song my dad wrote for us?" Lark asked.

"Why not?" Bill said with a grin. "How often does a first-time band get to play a song that a rock star wrote just for them?"

Lark started biting her thumbnail. Uh-oh. I knew what that meant. Lark always did that whenever she was worried.

The last time Lark sang her dad's song, in round number two, she was so nervous about pleasing him that she totally choked. She could barely get the words out of her mouth!

"Is it okay with you, Lark?" I asked.

"Sure." Lark shrugged. "Let's go for it."

I stood up and paced the room. "The song is called 'Butterfly Kiss,'" I said. "So what kind of dance number should we do?"

"I know!" Janelle said. "How about if we go outside and catch real butterflies? Then we can let them fly around the theater while we sing!"

"That reminds me of a scary movie I once saw," Lark said. "Millions of butterflies invaded this town. There were so many they started carrying off dogs and babies – "

Janelle groaned. "Next idea!"

I closed my eyes and thought of butterflies. When Ashley and I were around eight we caught a caterpillar and kept it in a jar. Days later the fuzzy-looking worm turned into a beautiful butterfly. "Hey!" I said. "Why don't we first flash pictures of caterpillars on the stage?"

Lark wrinkled her nose. "Caterpillars?" she repeated.

"Then what?" Janelle asked.

I pictured the whole thing in my head. "We can borrow a fog machine to make the stage look dreamy," I said. "Then the three of us can burst out onstage wearing colorful butterfly wings and funky makeup!"

"I like it, I like it," Lark said, nodding.

"And I can put gold streaks in my hair!" Janelle said.

I smiled at Janelle. She puts different-colored streaks in her hair for every round. Luckily they wash out!

"What do you think, Bill?" I asked.

"I think you totally rock, Mary-Kate," Bill said. "No wonder Rodney Beecham picked you to star in his TV special!"

Lark's smile turned into a frown. My stomach clenched when I saw her expression.

The door swung open. The camp owner, Stella Vickers, bopped into the room. She was dressed in cropped black pants and a red silk jacket. Her lips and nails were bright red, too.

"Guess what, Mary-Kate?" Stella exclaimed. "*Fave Rave* magazine wants to do a story about the lucky girl Rodney Beecham picked to star in his TV special!"

Did I just hear right? I wondered. *Fave Rave magazine only interviews teen celebrities – and now they want to interview me? Me? How awesome is that?*

"Mary-Kate!" Janelle whispered. "Didn't you tell Rodney that you weren't doing the special?"

I shook my head.

Twist and Shout

Diary, I'm so confused. What had started out as a dream come true was now turning into a big fat nightmare! Now, I not only have to tell Rodney I'm backing out, I have to tell Stella and *Fave Rave* magazine!

Things just got a lot more complicated.

Dear Diary,

This morning while everyone was in the music building talking about dance numbers and costumes, I was in the bunk, writing. No, not a new song for Electric Pink. An apology letter to Phoebe.

There was just one problem. I didn't have a clue where to send it!

The door flew open and Erin walked in. She was wearing pink shorts and a pink ruffled tank top – both from the May issue of *Teen Scene*.

"Ashley, why didn't you show up to talk about our dance number?" Erin asked. "We still have a great chance of winning Best Band. We got a score of nine out of ten in the last round, remember?"

But the only thing I remembered about that round was how Erin changed the words to Phoebe's song without telling us. And how I told Phoebe to forget about it. *Big* mistake!

"I can't stop thinking about Phoebe," I admitted. "I wrote an apology letter, but I don't know where to send it."

"Do you think this is *my* fault, Ashley?" Erin asked. "Do you think Phoebe left camp because I didn't listen to her ideas?"

"I didn't listen to her ideas, either, Erin," I admitted. "Maybe it's both of our faults."

Erin sat on the bed next to me and stared down at her sneakers.

"Look, Erin," I said, "in case Phoebe does come back, let's make a deal. Let's not be so quick to say bad things. Let's love one another's ideas for at least ten minutes. Okay?"

"Okay," Erin said. "And if Phoebe does come back, I promise I'll stay out of the way."

"Stay out of the way?" I said. "What do you mean?"

Erin shrugged. "You'd rather be friends with Phoebe than with me," she said. "That's okay. I can deal with it."

It was *not* okay! "Erin, I want us *all* to be friends," I said. "It's what I wanted from the beginning."

Erin's blue eyes opened wide. "Really?" she asked. "I thought you'd pick Phoebe over me because you've been friends for so long."

I shook my head. "No way. I really like you, too. I just wish that you and Phoebe could like each other."

"In that case, come on," Erin said. She grabbed my hand and pulled me off the bed. "And bring your letter."

"Where are we going?" I asked.

Erin flashed a big smile. "To find Phoebe!"

We headed for the camp office. Gloria Stevens, Stella's secretary, was sitting at her desk. She had short black curly hair and big green eyes. Her lips were covered with dark purple lipstick.

"Hi, Gloria," Erin said.

We stood in the doorway while Gloria tacked another picture of Bryan Leland on her bulletin board. Bryan was the cute singer of Kooky Melon. Gloria had about a dozen pictures of Bryan on her bulletin board. One had a purple lip print on it!

"Are you here for Phoebe Cahill's address again?" Gloria asked. "I told you, Ashley. I can't give you her address. It's private information."

Gloria moved her computer screen so it didn't face me. Was Phoebe's information on that screen right now?

"We wanted to tell you that we just saw Bryan Leland," Erin said. "Going into Stella's office."

We did? I glanced down the hall to Stella's office. *Why didn't I notice?*

"Bryan is here? Here?" Gloria gasped.

"Sure," Erin said. "Stella knows all the major rock stars."

Gloria jumped up. She ran to the door and turned toward Stella's office.

"Gloria!" Erin said quickly. "You've got lipstick all over your teeth. Maybe you'd better go to the ladies' room and look in the mirror."

"Thanks!" Gloria said, turning the other way.

"And take your time!" Erin called after her. "You want to look your best for Bryan."

I grabbed Erin's hand. "What are we waiting for?" I asked. "I want to meet Bryan Leland, too!"

"Bryan isn't here," Erin whispered. "I just said that so we could lose Gloria!"

Erin quickly sat down at Gloria's desk and looked at the screen. "Are we lucky or what?" she squealed. "Gloria was just about to send an e-mail to Phoebe's aunt!"

Erin positioned her hands on the keyboard. "Quick, Ashley," she said. "Read me your letter to Phoebe."

I stared at Erin. What she wanted to do didn't seem right. "No, Erin," I said. "We can't – "

Erin cut me off. "Do you want to apologise to Phoebe or not?" she asked.

"Of course!" I said.

"Then read!" Erin ordered.

I yanked out the letter and I began to read out loud: "'Dear Phoebe, when I discovered you left camp, it was one of the worst days of my whole life. I don't blame you for being mad – '"

"Faster!" Erin said.

Faster? I took a deep breath and blurted everything out as fast as I could. "'I should have listened to you when you tried to talk to me. And most of all, I never should have broken the promise I made to you before we came to camp.'"

I stopped to take another breath. I froze when I heard footsteps in the hall.

"Someone's coming!" Erin said.

"Keep typing!" I urged. Then I read: "'I miss you, Phoebe. So please forgive me. And please come back to camp. Your best friend forever, Ashley.'"

The footsteps were getting louder. I shoved the letter back in my pocket. Erin stood up and clicked on Send. She moved away from the desk just as the door flew open.

"H-hi, Gloria," I stammered.

"Don't 'hi' me!" Gloria snapped. She planted her hands on her hips. "Stella said that Bryan was *never* here!"

"Oh, no!" Erin gasped. She swayed back and forth. "Then I must be seeing . . . rock stars!"

I tried not to giggle as I placed my hand on Erin's forehead. "You'd better get that checked out," I said.

We ran out of the main building, laughing the whole way.

"I can't believe it!" I said. "How did you learn to type so fast, Erin?"

"By having over a hundred friends on my buddy list!" Erin said. She put her arm around my shoulder. "Now Phoebe will definitely get your apology letter."

Oh, Diary, I sure hope so!

Chapter 3

Saturday

Dear Diary,

The butterfly wings Janelle, Lark, and I made in the arts and crafts cabin this morning are amazing. The paper we used is so thin, it's practically see-through. And the silver glitter and sequins add the perfect touch!

"How am I going to play my guitar in these things?" Janelle asked as we tried on the wings.

"Why don't you just . . . wing it?" I joked.

Ashley and Erin were in the arts and crafts cabin, too. Erin was stringing pink beads to make necklaces for their band. Ashley is great at costume design, so she was helping me with my wings.

"I've been thinking, Mary-Kate," Ashley whispered as she fitted me with my wings. "Maybe you shouldn't bail out of the TV special."

"Yeah," Janelle said. "What if Rodney still doesn't ask Lark to sing with him? Then it'll all be a big waste."

We stopped talking when Lark walked over.

"Guess what, Mary-Kate?" Lark said. "I heard on the radio that my dad is going on a European tour sometime around Christmas. Maybe you'll get to go, too."

227

"Why me?" I asked.

"Because you're going to be on his TV special," Lark said. "My dad sometimes tours with people who perform with him."

"Europe? Really?" I could see myself banging on my buckets, cans, and basins in front of Big Ben in London, the Eiffel Tower in Paris, the Colosseum in Rome. . . .

"I've never been to Europe before," I said.

"Me neither," Lark said.

I snapped out of my daydream and stared at Lark. "Didn't you ever go on tour with your dad?" I asked.

Lark shook her head. "He never asked me."

My butterfly wings sagged. How could I think of touring with Rodney when he'd never even asked his own daughter?

That did it. I left the arts and crafts cabin and headed straight to Stella's office.

"Can I help you, Mary-Kate?" Stella asked. She was watering the plants in her office. "Or should I say . . . Madame Butterfly?"

Whoops. I forgot I was still wearing wings! "I need to call Rodney Beecham about the TV special, please," I said. "Is this a good time?"

Stella's eyes lit up. "It's always a good time for Rodney," she said. "Let me give you his number."

Stella opened her black address book. She wrote a telephone number on a sticky note and handed it to me. "I only have the number of his hotel in New York City," she said.

Someone knocked on the door. A counselor poked her head in. "Stella?" she said. "A camper just got her braces stuck on her trumpet mouthpiece!"

"Oh, great!" Stella moaned. "This is the second time this summer we've had a braces emergency!" She ran out of her office.

I picked up the receiver and dialed the number. "Metropolis Hotel," a man answered. "This is Jay."

"Hi," I said. "I'd like to speak to Rodney Beecham, please."

"You and a million other girls," Jay said. "Sorry. Mr. Beecham isn't taking any calls from fans."

"But I'm not a fan!" I exclaimed. "I mean . . . I am, but that's not why I'm calling. I'm performing in Rodney's next TV special."

"Right!" Jay laughed. "And I'm starring in Jennifer Lopez's next movie!"

Click.

I stared at the receiver. Jay had hung up!

I dialed the number one more time. When Jay answered again, I blurted out, "Jay, you've got to listen to me. Rodney Beecham *asked* me to be in his TV special – "

"You again?" Jay groaned. "Nice try. But it's not going to work."

Click.

"Great," I muttered. "How can I tell Rodney I can't do the TV special if I can't talk to him?"

Dear Diary,

Sunday morning I poured orange juice on my cornflakes. No, it's not some weird new health-kick. It's because I was tired from being up all night wondering if Phoebe got my e-mail. If she did, would she ever write me back? And if so, when? And what would she say?

If that wasn't enough – it's just three days away from round number three, and Erin and I still haven't decided on a dance number. Can things get any worse?

"All the other bands have their choreography numbers worked out," Jennifer said at practice. "What do we have so far? Zero. Zip. Zilch!"

Erin stared down at the ground. I felt bad, too. Up until then I'd had Phoebe on the brain – not music.

Twist and Shout

Jennifer is right, I thought. *We have to come up with something.*

I kicked my brain into gear. "Check this out," I said. I turned on our radio boom box and found a pulsing techno-beat. Erin watched as I demonstrated moves from my dance class at school. I hopped from side to side, pumping my arms and legs in the air.

Erin tried copying me. "My knee keeps cracking," she complained.

"Then try this," I said as I fell into a split.

"As if!" Erin cried. "I definitely do not move that way."

I sighed. We couldn't win the choreography round if we didn't have a dance number. Any dance number!

"Okay," I said. "Let's go with *your* dance idea."

"You mean you'll shake it up?" Erin asked.

"Sure," I said, standing up.

"Okay." Jennifer pulled a stopwatch from her pocket. "First let's plan out some dance steps so I can time them."

"Okay!" Erin said. "Stand right next to me, Ashley, and do exactly as I do."

I watched Erin as she began to dance. "Let your hips sway and your arms jerk," Erin said.

I feel like a jerk, I thought as I copied her.

"Next, bend your head way, way over," Erin said. "As if you were a floppy rag doll."

I bent all the way forward – just like I do when I brush knots out of my hair!

"Now sway your head back and forth," Erin said. "And don't forget to make eye contact with the judges."

"Eye contact?" I laughed. "How can I with all this hair in my face?"

Erin straightened up. "Don't you like my dance number, Ashley?" she asked.

"It's not that I don't *like* it, Erin," I said, straightening up, too. "It's just that it's so . . . so . . . "

"Bubble-gummy?" a voice asked behind me.

Who said that?

I turned my head and gasped. Standing at the door with a big grin on her face was – "*Phoebe?*"

Chapter 4

Sunday

Dear Diary,

"Phoebe!" I shouted.

"Ashley!" Phoebe shouted.

We raced to each other with open arms.

"I'm sorry!" we both said at the same time.

I looked at Phoebe. "Why are *you* sorry?" I asked. "I'm the one who broke my promise. Not you."

"I know," Phoebe said. "But I spoke to my aunt Marie about everything that happened. She told me the promise you made was much too big to keep. I shouldn't have expected you to hang out with no one but me."

"But I should have known how upset you were," I said.

Phoebe shook her head. "And I should have made sure you knew how I truly felt," she said. "Instead of just leaving."

Then Phoebe looked straight at Erin.

Uh-oh, I thought. *What if Phoebe is still mad at Erin?*

"Erin, I'm sorry I blamed you for putting that red sock in my wash," Phoebe said. "When I spoke to my mom, she said she'd packed a pair of red socks in my duffel bag. The sock that turned my clothes pink was really mine."

"No way!" Erin exclaimed.

"It's true." Phoebe laughed.

"Are you back at camp now, Phoebe? For good?" I asked.

Phoebe nodded. "I missed you guys," she said. "And besides," she added with a grin, "my aunt Marie has six cats that kept me up all night."

"Okay, okay," Jennifer said. "Now that we've had our warm and fuzzy moment, can we please choose a dance number?"

Erin looked Phoebe up and down. "Not until Phoebe tells me where she got that awesome dress," she said.

Phoebe glanced down at her white minidress. It had a tomato soup can print on it. "This dress is vintage nineteen sixty-six," she said. "My aunt lent me tons of sixties clothes to bring back to camp."

"How did she get them?" I asked.

"Aunt Marie wore all kinds of mod clothes when she danced on *American Grandstand*," Phoebe explained.

Erin gaped at Phoebe. "That is so cool. *American Grandstand* was the hottest teen show in history."

"And look at the dance steps Aunt Marie showed me," Phoebe said. She moved her hands as if she were climbing a tree. "This is called the Monkey."

Phoebe showed us how to dance the Skate, the Shingaling, and the Mashed Potato. Somewhere in the middle of the Philly Dog, I got the most amazing idea! "Hey, you guys," I said. "Why don't we turn Electric Pink into Electric Pink a Go-Go?"

"Electric Pink . . . a go-go?" Erin repeated.

"The mod look is hot this year," I explained. "And we still haven't decided on a dance number, so – "

"So let's go totally sixties!" Phoebe cried.

"Sweet!" Erin said.

"We can sing a song from the sixties, wear sixties clothes, and do a bunch of dances from the sixties, too," I suggested.

"I'll call my mom," Erin said. "Maybe she can mail us some old issues of *Teen Scene* magazine. So we can see what hairstyles and makeup girls wore back then."

Jennifer loved the idea, too. She offered to flash psychedelic designs on the wall while we performed.

"Wait," Erin said, looking at her watch. "We're supposed to love one another's ideas for ten minutes."

"All I need is ten *seconds*," I said.

"Me too!" Phoebe said. "I love it."

"Great," Erin said.

"You mean *groovy*!" I giggled.

Phoebe, Erin, and I spent the whole afternoon planning our dances and our new look. But the best part is, Diary, everyone is getting along. *At last!*

Dear Diary,

This afternoon, Janelle and I had a few minutes alone in our bunk.

"I have to get out of that music special," I said. I told her about my failed phone call with Jay earlier. "But how *can* I when I can't reach Rodney?"

"Of course you can't reach Rodney Beecham," Janelle said. "He's a superstar."

"Then who else can I try to call?" I asked.

Janelle tightened her guitar strings as she thought. "What about Rodney's manager?" she suggested. "The one who came with Rodney when he visited the camp last time?"

Of course! My forehead wrinkled as I tried to remember the woman's name. "Dorothy . . . Dolly . . ." I snapped my fingers. "Doris! Her name is Doris! She gave me her business card with her phone number in case I had any questions."

"Perfect!" Janelle said. "Where is it?"

"I think I stuck it in my jeans pocket," I said, reaching into my pocket. Nothing. "I guess I was wearing my other jeans that day. The ones I put in my laundry bag."

Janelle pointed out the window. "You mean the one going to the laundry today?" she asked.

"Huh?" I glanced out the window. A guy with a cap was loading the campers' laundry bags into a big truck.

"Janelle!" I squeaked. "I have to get Doris's card back. Before it shreds in the wash!"

I raced out of the bunk. "Stop!" I shouted as I ran after the truck. "I left something in my pocket!"

I wasn't alone. Mandy Plotnick was chasing the truck right behind me. Mandy had left her favorite lip gloss in her pocket.

We stopped running as the truck drove out of the camp gate. We stared after it, panting.

"There goes my only tube of Cherry-Berry," Mandy said.

And there goes Doris's phone number – and my only chance to reach Rodney I thought.

As I trudged back to the bunk I dug my hands into the pockets of my hoodie. That's when I felt something. It was stiff like cardboard and rectangular like a business card.

A business card?

Hey, wait a minute, I thought.

I pulled out the card and smiled. It *was* Doris's business card and telephone number!

Am I lucky or what? I thought. *I guess I never put it in my jeans after all. Now let's see if I'm lucky enough to reach Doris – and get out of the TV special!*

Chapter 5

Monday

Dear Diary,

You should have seen us this morning. Electric Pink arrived in the practise room wearing the clothes we chose for the round tomorrow. Phoebe wore an orange vinyl miniskirt with a matching vinyl jacket. Erin picked out a black sleeveless dress splashed with yellow and white daisies, and daisy-shaped earrings, too. I'm wearing white bell-bottom hip-hugger pants and a cropped red jacket.

"You guys are stylin'!" Jennifer said. "Erin, I love those mod daisies on your dress."

"So do the bees." Erin groaned. "They chased me all the way here."

We all gathered around the stereo to choose a song. After listening to tons of CDs of sixties music, we decided on a tune called "Twist and Shout."

"Let's *dance* the Twist, too," Phoebe said.

"How do you do that?" I asked.

"You just twist at the waist," Phoebe said. "And grind your foot on the floor like you're stepping on a bug!"

"Ewww!" Erin said with a giggle.

"You guys stay here and practise," Jennifer said. "I'll look into some special effects."

As Jennifer pulled the door open, Skye Martell, Tori Seever, and Abigail Bederman from the band Venus fell into the room. They were wearing silver space suits and space boots.

"Were you guys listening in?" Jennifer demanded. "It's not cool for bands to spy on other bands."

"You're Jennifer, aren't you?" Skye asked. "Your guitar playing *rules*. No wonder they call you Guitar Goddess!"

Jennifer's face softened. "Thanks."

Then Skye lowered her voice and said, "Don't tell our instructor, Tina, but we really wish *you* were our instructor."

"That is so sweet," Jennifer gushed. She left the room, and the girls from Venus strolled over to us.

They weren't smiling sweetly anymore.

"Hi," I said. "I'm Ashley. This is Phoebe. And Erin."

"We know," Abigail said.

"Let's cut to the chase," Skye said. "You may be ahead of us, but not for long."

I blinked hard. "Excuse me?"

Skye flipped her long red hair over her shoulder. "We're the real deal," she said. "We sound better than you, have better costumes than you, and we probably dance better than you, too!"

"*And* we're using a bubble machine for special effects," Tori said, her dark eyes flashing.

"Can you top that?" Abigail asked with a mean grin. "I don't think so!"

Diary, I couldn't believe my ears. Were these girls snooty or what?

"Don't think you're such hot stuff, Electric Pink," Skye said. "Venus is going to win the Battle of the Bands – no matter *what* it takes."

Venus left the room and slammed the door. Erin, Phoebe, and I turned to one another, our mouths open in shock.

"Who do they think they are?" Phoebe cried.

"Why did they say all those nasty things about our band?" Erin exclaimed.

"Who knows?" I said. "Unless they're trying to psych us out."

"Psych us out?" Phoebe asked nervously. "I don't get it."

"Venus is getting nervous because they know we're good," I explained. "That's why they're trying to scare us. So we don't do well in the next rounds."

"Scare us?" Phoebe cried. "Hah!"

"Let them try," Erin declared. "Nobody scares Electric Pink."

The three of us high-fived with knuckles. Knuckles meant business. Then we all shouted, "Electric Pink rules!"

And with our groovy sixties costumes and cool song, we are going to *prove* it!

Dear Diary,

This morning after breakfast I raced to Stella's office to call Doris.

"When you talk to Rodney's manager," Stella said as I sat down, "ask her if Rodney can mention Camp Rock 'n' Roll in his song."

Oh, great, I thought. *Stella really wants the camp to be a part of Rodney's TV special. How can I get out of it with her listening in? I can't kick her out of her own office.*

The door flew open, and an instructor rushed in. "Stella, one of the bands is planning on using pyrotechnics!" he said.

"You mean *fire*?" Stella gasped. "Absolutely not! Once I finish with Mary-Kate, I'll come and set them straight."

"No!" I blurted. "I'm fine by myself. Really!"

"Really?" Stella asked.

"Really," I said firmly.

"Well, okay, then," Stella said, standing up.

Stella and the instructor hurried out of the office. I pulled out Doris's card and dialed the number. After a few rings – "Doris Gavin here!" a voice snapped.

"Um, Doris," I said. "This is Mary-Kate Burke. I just wanted to – "

"Mary-Kate!" Doris interrupted. "I was just going to call you. I need your dad's name for the release form."

"It's Kevin. Kevin Burke," I said. "But I really need to talk to you. It's about the TV special."

"Oh, we're excited, too, Mary-Kate," Doris said. "Hold on – I have a call on another line."

An old Rodney Beecham song came on the line while Doris put me on hold. I was just starting to hum it when –

"I'm back," Doris chirped. "Now, what did you want to tell me, Mary-Kate?"

I took a deep breath and said, "I don't think I can do the TV special, Doris. You see – "

"Sure you can do it," Doris cut in. "You have just the right energy. Rats – there's my other line again."

"Wait!" I said. But Doris put me on hold – again!

A different Rodney Beecham song came on. But I didn't want to listen to music. I wanted to get out of the TV special once and for all.

"Me again," Doris said. "That was Rodney's yoga instructor. He wanted to know how many sticky mats he should bring on our next tour. As if I care."

"Doris – " I started to say.

"I'll mail that release form to your dad ASAP, Mary-Kate," Doris said. "And we'll see you when we come up to camp next week for the TV shoot. Bye, now."

Click.

I can't believe it! I thought. *Getting out of a rock TV special is just as hard as getting into one!*

I stuffed Doris's card back into my pocket and wondered if it was worth calling her back later. As I walked out of the main building, Janelle ran over.

"So?" Janelle asked. "Did you do it? Are you out?"

"No." I sighed. "Rodney's manager is too busy to talk. And I'm sure I still won't be able to get to Rodney, either."

"Maybe what you need is a password," Janelle said.

"A what?" I said.

"Rodney's secret password," Janelle said. "Sometimes it's the only way to get through to a famous rocker."

"How do you know?" I asked.

"I've been trying to call Jim Nolan of Gag Reflex for about a year," Janelle said. "No luck."

Janelle pulled a notepad and pen from her guitar case. She put the case on the ground and got ready to write. "If Rodney Beecham had a secret password," she said, tapping her chin with her pen, "what would it be?"

"Rodney's last CD was called *Poison Ivy*," I said.

"Poison ivy!" Janelle began to write. "Itch . . . scratch . . . rash. Rash! What a cool name for our band! Itchy Rash – "

"Janelle," I cut in. "Focus."

"Sorry," Janelle said. "Rodney did a cereal commercial once."

"Cereal," I said. "Crunchy . . . flaky . . . milky . . . "

"He has a dog," Janelle added. "Bark . . . fetch . . . stay!"

I know what you're thinking, Diary. Guessing Rodney Beecham's secret password won't exactly be a piece of cake.

Hey, wait a minute. Cake . . . cupcake . . . cookie . . . I'd better add those to my list!

Chapter 6

Tuesday

Dear Diary,

This is it! Round three – choreography! Phoebe, Erin, and I spent the whole morning putting on sixties makeup and teasing our hair to the max.

"When do I stop?" I asked, fluffing my hair with a fine-tooth comb.

"When it reaches the ceiling," Phoebe joked.

Erin showed us how to paint our eyelids with liquid eyeliner. Next we borrowed some of Erin's pale pink and white lipstick. They were the "rage" back in the sixties.

"How did you get all this cool retro makeup, Erin?" Phoebe asked.

Erin smiled at us with pink pearly lips. "Not only does my mom get me free clothes from *Teen Scene* magazine, she gets me free makeup," she said. "And free hair stuff. And free nail polish. And a free subscription – "

"We get the picture." I giggled.

I blotted my lipstick with a tissue, then gave myself one last look. Ready! "Let's hurry," I said, "or we'll be late!"

Twist and Shout

We grabbed our instruments and raced to the camp theater. Jennifer waved to us from the aisle. "Good luck!" she called. "I'll be up in the lighting booth working the special effects."

I knew what the special effects would be: pink and black spirals all over the stage wall. Very psychedelic!

A few guys called "roadies" were already up on the stage. Their job was to set up all the amps, microphones, and instruments before each band played.

"Welcome, rockers!" Stella said as she walked across the stage with a handheld microphone. "Today's round is all about choreography!"

Everyone cheered.

"But first, let's give it up for our judges," Stella said. "Clarence Meekins, Sophie Amir, and Terrence Boyle!"

The judges waved from their table.

Sophie looked her totally glam self in a black sleeveless dress and huge silver hoop earrings. Clarence was wearing his usual backward baseball cap. Sophie and Clarence are tough judges but always have something nice to say. Then there's Terrence. Terrence "the Terror" Boyle is known for being honest. A little *too* honest!

"The first band up will be Fresh Start," Stella said. "Girls, the stage is yours!"

The three girls of Fresh Start hurried onstage. One sat down behind a set of drums. One stood at a keyboard. Another picked up a trumpet.

After an opening drum solo, Fresh Start began to sing: "'I want candy! I want candy!'"

When they weren't singing or playing their instruments, Fresh Start wowed us with their awesome moves. Their legs and arms moved in perfect sync. One girl spun on her head so fast, she became a blur!

Fresh Start got huge cheers. And high scores from Clarence and Sophie. But as for Terrence . . .

"If this were a gymnastics competition, I would have given you a ten," he said. "But since you all sang flat, you get a five from me. Sorry."

"Ouch!" Phoebe whispered.

"Thanks, Fresh Start," Stella said. "Now let's put on our space gear and blast off to Planet Venus!"

"Venus!" Phoebe whispered. "Let's see if they're as good as they say they are."

First Skye, Tori, and Abigail moonwalked across the stage. Next they broke into their robotic dance steps. Then they played their instruments while pictures of planets and stars flashed all over the theater. The bubble machine was a big hit, too.

"'Cosmic Cutie up so far, send me your love on a shooting star!'" they sang.

"I'm pretty sure the judges won't like it," Erin whispered. "Whoever heard of bubbles in space?"

The judges *did* like it. A lot. They gave Venus a *nine*! One point away from a perfect ten!

"All riiight!" Stella said. "Now let's get back to Earth and hear from the gals of Electric Pink a Go-Go!"

"I can't believe we have to go after Venus," Phoebe whispered. "They were so good."

"So are *we*!" I whispered back.

Phoebe, Erin, and I walked onto the stage. Once we were set up, Jennifer gave us a thumbs-up from the projection booth.

"One, two," Erin called out. "One, two, three!"

Phoebe and I strummed our guitars and began to sing, "'Shake it up, baby, now. Twist and shout. Twist and shout!'"

After a few minutes our recorded music began to play. It was our cue to dance!

Phoebe and I put down our guitars. Erin stepped away from her keyboard. The three of us danced the Monkey, the Skate, and the Jerk. I was just about to switch to the Mashed Potato when pink and black spirals swirled all over the stage. I tried to keep dancing, but all those swirling lights were making me dizzy. Soon it felt as if the whole stage were swirling – faster and faster and faster!

Diary, I could barely feel the floor under my feet. My eyes started to cross. My stomach started to churn.

Omigosh! I thought in a panic. *I'm going to barf!*

Dear Diary,

I didn't know what to do! There I was, sitting in the third row of the theater, watching my sister turn a sickly shade of green! "Ashley is going to hurl," I whispered to Lark.

"Oh, no!" Lark gasped.

"Are you going to do something?" Janelle whispered.

Just then, Jennifer switched the effects to giant mod hearts and daisies. Luckily they didn't swirl! Phew!

Ashley made it through the whole song, and Electric Pink got a score of nine from the judges!

"That's what I call moving to the groove," Clarence said. "Good job, Electric Pink."

"For a minute there I thought I was back in the sixties," Sophie said. "You girls were on fire."

Twist and Shout

"Your swaying was very dramatic, too, Ashley," Terrence said. "Nice touch. Very nice touch."

I looked at my friends and cracked a smile.

Stella tallied the judges' scores. "All riiiight!" she declared. "Electric Pink gets a nine, too!"

After two more bands it was time for Crush.

"Let's do it!" Janelle said.

Wearing our butterfly wings and glittery makeup, we slipped behind the stage curtain. We waited while Bill projected shots of squirmy caterpillars all over the stage. The roadies worked the fog machine, creating a fine mist. Janelle strummed a chord, and we burst through the curtain.

"'When you're away, the thing I miss,'" Lark sang. "'Is your great smile and your butterfly kiss!'"

Diary, we gave it all we got. But when our song was over, the judges only gave us six points.

"So what if our wings kept knocking together?" Janelle complained later in the bunk. "It didn't bother me."

"Well, it bothered the judges," I said as I started taking off my glitter makeup.

"So did our pictures of the caterpillars," Janelle said. "I heard Terrence tell Sophie that caterpillars gross him out."

"Spiders gross my dad out," Lark said.

I froze with the cotton ball in my hand. Could "spider" be Rodney's secret password? "Spiders, huh?" I said slowly. "Are there any other bugs your dad doesn't like?"

"Not that I know of," Lark said.

"Any bugs he *loves*?" I asked. "How about ladybugs? Does he have a favourite animal? A favourite ice-cream flavor?"

"No," Lark said, staring at me.

Janelle shot me a grin. She must have known I was still trying to figure out Rodney's password. But Lark didn't have a clue.

"Are you okay, Mary-Kate?" Lark asked. "You've been acting kind of weird these last few days."

"Actually, I could use some fresh air," I said. "I'll be right back!"

I grabbed Rodney's New York telephone number, my list of passwords, and raced to Stella's office.

"*Another* call to Rodney Beecham?" Stella asked when she saw me. She shrugged. "Go ahead."

I dialed the number as fast as I could.

"Metropolis Hotel," a voice answered. "Jay speaking."

It's Jay, I thought. *The same guy from a few days ago.*

"Can I help you?" Jay asked.

"Um – spider?" I blurted. "Spider *web* . . . tarantula . . . creepy crawly . . . Little Miss Muffet . . . itchy . . . wire-haired terrier?"

"Is this some kind of joke?" Jay asked.

"No!" I cried. "Queen Elizabeth . . . pistachio?"

Click.

"He did it again," I wailed. "He hung up."

I forgot I wasn't alone. I looked up and saw Stella staring at me. "Is everything okay, Mary-Kate?" she asked.

"Fine," I said, forcing a smile. "Everything's fine."

But I knew it wasn't.

Lark should be doing this TV special. But it looks like *I'm* doing it – whether I want to or not!

Chapter 7

Wednesday

Dear Diary,

Because we worked so hard on the last round, Stella gave us the whole day off. That meant no practise or music classes. Some campers practiced with their bands, anyway. Some slept late and just relaxed.

Phoebe, Erin, and I did both. We hung out by the lake, but we practiced guitar chords and talked about the next round. The *final* round!

"We showed those girls from Venus," Erin said. She leaned back against a tree. "We were as good as they were."

"Better!" Phoebe said.

"Let's forget about Venus and think about the next round," I said. "I say we stick with the sixties look. That went over big."

"Thanks to Phoebe," Erin said with a smile.

I smiled, too, as I strummed my guitar. It was supercool to have us all get along!

"The final round focuses on songwriting," I said. "Should we start coming up with a new song?"

"We don't have to," Phoebe said. She pulled a piece of paper from her guitar case. "I just happen to have a new song right here."

"What a surprise!" I joked. Phoebe had been writing songs nonstop since she got to camp.

"This song is kind of serious, but in a fun way," Phoebe said. "It's called 'Great to Know You.'"

"What's it about?" Erin asked.

"It's about opening your heart to new people," Phoebe explained.

New people? I thought. *As in . . . Erin?*

Phoebe strummed her guitar as she sang. When she was finished, she looked up and said, "What do you think?"

She glanced nervously at Erin.

Uh-oh, I thought. *What if Erin doesn't like it? What if Phoebe and Erin start fighting again?*

Erin grinned. "I love it!" she said.

"You do?" Phoebe asked.

"What a *relief!*" I cried. I quickly shook my head. "I mean – what a coincidence – I love it, too!"

"It's great to sing about friends," Erin said. "We can even flash pictures of new friends here at Camp Rock 'n' Roll!"

"This time we should wear go-go boots," Phoebe said. "They're little white boots that all the cool girls wore in the sixties. I think I saw some in the costume cabin."

"What are we waiting for?" I asked. We raced to the costume cabin.

Linda, the costume counselor, was busy ironing The Corral Chicks' denim skirts. She looked totally cool in khaki flared pants, a black tank top, and colored bangles up to her elbows. Linda put aside her iron and helped us pick out three pink minidresses and three pairs of white go-go boots.

"I've never worn vintage boots," Erin said. "What if the girl who wore these before had sweaty feet?"

"Mod girls in the sixties never sweated," Phoebe joked. "They were too cool!"

"Good one," a voice said behind us.

I spun around. Skye, Tori, and Abigail were walking into the cabin.

Venus!

"Those boots are so slammin'!" Skye said. "Are you wearing them in the next round?"

I kept my mouth shut because I didn't trust them. Were they here to put down our band again?

"They are so perfect for your look," Skye said. "But then everything Linda picks out is perfect."

"You think?" Linda said.

"For sure!" Tori said. "In fact, we were just going to ask you if you have any bracelets we can wear."

"Come to think of it," Linda said. "I think I have some silver bracelets in the back room."

"We'll wait," Tori said sweetly.

When Linda was in the back, the girls of Venus stopped smiling.

"Okay, we tied for that last round," Skye said. "But you were just lucky."

"The *next* round is what really counts," Abigail said.

I shrugged. "May the best band win," I said.

"And that is going to be us!" Skye said. "We're older than you. And we're better than you, too."

"*And* we have a bubble machine!" Tori said. She stuck out her tongue like a little kid!

The three girls walked into the back room. Phoebe, Erin, and I exchanged stunned looks.

"Are they super mean or what?" Erin asked.

"Should we tell somebody?" Phoebe asked.

I thought about it, but shook my head. "They didn't really do anything to us," I said. "Besides being nasty."

"Thanks, Linda!" Skye's voice boomed from the back. "These bracelets are perfect. You *are* a fashion-genius!"

"And you guys are so sweet," Linda's voice gushed.

I rolled my eyes.

Skye, Tori, and Abigail were kissing up to the instructors and the counselors. No one had any idea what Venus was *really* like!

"Even if we did complain to the counselors and instructors about Venus," I said, "who would believe us?"

Dear Diary,

After practicing our new song, Janelle took her guitar outside. Lark and I stayed in the bunk to write some letters.

"I'm almost done. How about a game of football?" Lark asked.

"Sounds great!" I licked my last envelope and tossed it aside. I noticed a book on Lark's bedside table.

"What are you reading?" I asked, nodding toward the book.

Lark held it up for me to see. A picture of Rodney Beecham was on the cover. The title of the book was *Rodney Beecham: Feed Me with Rock!* "It's my dad's autobiography," Lark said. "It came in the mail yesterday." She tossed it to me.

"Wow!" I said, opening the book. "He even signed it for you."

"Big deal," Lark said. "I'd rather get to know my dad in person than in some book. And do you believe there's just one paragraph about me? One dumb paragraph!"

Diary, I couldn't take it anymore. Lark's dad was making her so miserable.

"Why don't you just get real with your dad, Lark?" I asked. "Tell him that you want to be in his TV special!"

"But I *don't* want to be in the TV special," Lark said.

I stared at Lark. "You don't?"

"It's not about the music, Mary-Kate," Lark said. "It's about spending more time with my dad."

"It is?" I asked.

Lark nodded. "But maybe it's better that I hardly see him," she said. "He would probably think I was a drag."

"How can you be a drag?" I asked.

"My dad loves to perform. I don't," Lark explained. "He loves flashy clothes. I like T-shirts and jeans. He loves attention. I get shy around lots of people."

"In other words . . . you and your dad have nothing in common," I said.

"Zero!" Lark said.

While Lark looked for her sneakers, I flipped through Rodney's autobiography. As I was about to put the book on Lark's bed, it suddenly hit me: If I could help Lark connect with her dad, she would finally be happy.

And I'd be happy being in the TV special. We'd both get what we really want!

All I had to do was find something that they had in common.

"Can we play football later, Lark?" I asked. "I want to check out your dad's new book."

Lark's shoulders dropped. She looked disappointed. I wasn't sure if it was because she was looking forward to soccer, or because she was afraid I was becoming one of her dad's obsessed fans. But, I reminded myself, it was all for a good cause.

She shrugged. "Sure. Knock yourself out."

I carried the book outside. I found Janelle lying on the grass, bopping to the beat of her Walkman.

"Janelle!" I said, waving the book over her face. "Check it out!"

Janelle pulled off her headphones. Her eyes went wide as I explained everything.

"That's why I have to read Rodney's biography," I said. "It's the only way I'll find out what Rodney likes to do. And I hope Lark will like doing the same things."

Janelle whistled as she flipped through the book. "This book is three hundred and fifteen pages," she said.

"I've never read such a thick book before," I admitted.

"I can help you look through it," Janelle offered. "But if we're going to go through Rodney's whole life, we'd better get started. He's been around over forty years!"

I opened the book and flipped through the pages. "Check out these pictures in the middle," I said. I pointed to a shot of a woman holding a baby. They both had big dark eyes. "I'll bet that's Lark and her mom."

Janelle peered over my shoulder as I turned more pages. I stopped at a chapter called "The Great Outdoors" and read out loud: "'Being on tour for months can make a bloke batty. So when I get to my castle I pull on my hiking boots, whistle for my wire-haired terrier Oliver, and take long walks on my estate.'"

"What do you know?" Janelle said. "Rodney likes to hike."

"Janelle, that's it," I said, shutting the book. "Lark and her dad can go hiking together."

"Wait a minute," Janelle said, shaking her head. "How do you know if Lark even likes hiking?"

"I don't," I admitted. "But there's only one way to find out!"

Chapter 8

Later Wednesday

Dear Diary,

I know I already wrote you today, Diary, but I just have to tell you what happened.

It wasn't easy talking Lark into taking a hike. All she wanted to do was play football.

"I promise we'll play football after the hike," I said for the fourth time.

"Okay," Lark finally said. "But since when are you so into hiking?"

Gulp! I'd never been hiking in my life. So I had to think of something fast. "Um, this *is* the country," I said. "So why shouldn't we be one with nature? Or, in our case – two?"

It was late afternoon and getting cool. We pulled on our hoodies and headed for the woodsy part of camp.

"Shouldn't we bring a flashlight?" Lark asked as we entered the woods. "Or canteens?"

"Maybe we should drop breadcrumbs, too!" I joked. "These woods aren't that deep. And we won't be long."

I hope! I thought.

Twigs and leaves crunched under our sneakers

as we trekked into the woods. I could hear crickets chirping and birds twittering up in the trees.

"Hey! I have an idea. Maybe you can go hiking with your dad when he gets here," I said. "Wouldn't that be neat?"

"Are you serious?" Lark scoffed. "My dad hates the outdoors."

I stopped walking and stared at Lark. "He . . . what?" I asked.

"My dad hates the outdoors," Lark repeated. "He's always getting bitten by mosquitoes. He once even got poison ivy in his own backyard. Why do you think he named his last CD *Poison Ivy*?"

"But . . . the book said your dad loves hiking!" I said.

"The book lied," Lark said. She slapped her neck and started scratching. "Now I'm getting attacked by mosquitoes, too. Just great!"

I heard a loud snap. And a screech.

"What was that?" Lark whispered.

"Probably just nature sounds," I said.

Lark started scratching her leg. "I think I've had enough of nature," she said. "Can we go back to camp now?"

Boy, Diary, did I goof! Not only does Lark hate hiking – her dad does, too.

There's got to be something Rodney likes to do, I thought. *Something that doesn't call for flashlights or bug spray!*

Dear Diary,

This morning after arts and crafts, Phoebe, Erin, and I carried our new sixties outfits from the costume cabin to the music building. Each practice room has its own clothing rack so the bands don't have to keep their costumes in the bunks.

"I can't wait to show Jennifer our outfits," I said. "Especially the go-go boots. They are so stylin'."

We hung up our minidresses and lined up our boots against the wall. Then we headed to the mess hall for lunch. Our bunk counselor, Ivy, sat across from me. Instead of eating spaghetti and meatballs like the rest of us, she just nibbled on a roll.

"What's up, Ivy?" I asked. "Don't you feel well?"

"I have no appetite," Ivy said. "The girls from Venus left the most awesome cookies in the counselors' lounge this morning. Abigail's mom sent them in a care package."

Venus? I looked sideways at Phoebe and Erin.

"Those girls should win an award for the nicest band," Ivy said. "Don't you think?"

Twist and Shout

No one said a word. I glanced over at the next table. Abigail was winding her spaghetti on a fork. She looked right at me and smiled. A slow, sly smile. Then Skye speared a meatball on her fork and waved it back and forth.

"Why is she doing that?" Phoebe whispered.

"They're still trying to psych us out," I whispered. "Let's just ignore them."

After lunch, Bunk Elvis played a mean game of softball with Bunk Tina Turner. Mary-Kate scored two home runs! Then we all headed to the music building for band practice.

Jennifer was waiting for us in our music room. She pointed to the rack. "Amazing costumes," she said.

"Wait until you see the boots," I said.

We kicked off our sneakers and pulled off our bulky socks. Then we stuck our feet into the boots.

Squish!

"Ewww!" Phoebe cried.

"My boots have worms inside them!" Erin exclaimed.

"Worms?" Jennifer gasped.

Yick! My own boot was filled with some kind of cold, squishy, squiggly mush. Diary, I practically gagged – that's how grossed out I was!

We yanked our boots off and gasped. Our feet were covered with red and brown goop that smelled like meat sauce. When we tipped our boots over, clumps of spaghetti and meatballs plopped out on the floor.

"Gross!" I cried.

"Who would do this to our vintage go-go boots? Now they're totally ruined!" Phoebe wailed.

I remembered the look Abigail gave me in the mess hall while she was winding her spaghetti. And that meatball Skye waved at me. I had a pretty good idea who had dumped the spaghetti and meatballs into our boots. But Erin spoke up before I did.

"The girls from Venus have been acting pretty snooty lately," Erin said. "It must have been them."

Jennifer shook her head. "The girls from Venus are so sweet," she said. "They wouldn't do something like that."

"But – " Erin started to say.

"In fact," Jennifer went on, "Abigail helped me restring my guitar. She's good at it. And fast, too."

I groaned under my breath. It was no use. Venus had already kissed up to Jennifer!

"Do you want to report this prank to Stella?" Jennifer asked.

"That's okay," I said. "We'll deal with it."

Erin and Phoebe stared at me.

"Why don't you wash your feet while I take these boots to the costume cabin?" Jennifer said. "Maybe Linda can have them cleaned."

Phoebe, Erin, and I left meat sauce tracks in the hall as we walked to the bathroom.

"Ashley, why *don't* you want to tell Stella?" Phoebe asked. "We can't let Venus get away with this."

"We're Electric Pink – not Electric Rat Fink," I explained. "And we don't have any proof that Venus did it."

"Proof-shmoof." Erin narrowed her blue eyes. "We should get *even*. A prank for a prank, that's what I say!"

That didn't fly with me. Once we got even, Venus would do something to top us. And we would just go back and forth trying to get revenge.

"Getting even isn't what we're about," I said. "We'd only be stooping to their level."

I knew the Battle of the Bands would be tough. But I never dreamed it would be an all-out *war*!

Chapter 9

Friday

Dear Diary,

Today was the first rainy day at camp. So instead of the volleyball game and canoe lessons that were scheduled for this morning, the whole camp played Rock 'n' Roll bingo in the mess hall.

But not me! I stayed in the bunk and read about Rodney Beecham.

"I can't believe you talked me into missing Rock 'n' Roll bingo for this," Janelle said. "It's like doing homework."

We sat on my bed in Bunk Elvis, flipping through the book I held on my lap.

"I'm on a mission, Janelle," I said. "There *has* to be something Rodney likes that Lark likes, too."

"Hey," Janelle said, pointing to a page. "It says that Rodney is good at arm wrestling. Do you think Lark is good at that?"

I pictured Lark arm-wrestling the muscled roadies in the mess-hall. "I hope not!" I groaned.

I turned the page. The next chapter was called "Chip off the Ol' Rock-Block." It was about Rodney's father.

"According to this, Rodney's dad used to play the trumpet in his army band," I said.

Twist and Shout

"So?" Janelle asked. "We want to know what Rodney likes doing – not his dad."

"Wait," I said. "It also says that Rodney's dad used to take him rowing when he was a kid."

"He did?" Janelle asked.

I read the paragraph out loud: "'Rowing with my dad is one of my best memories. So whenever I feel low – all I have to do is *row*!'"

I looked up and stared at Janelle. "The camp has rowboats out on the lake," I said. "Maybe Lark can go rowing with her dad when he visits."

"Did you ever see Lark row before?" Janelle asked.

"No," I said. "But there's always a first time."

As soon as it stopped raining, I looked for Lark. I found her on the playing field dribbling a football. It was muddy, but Lark didn't seem to mind.

She kicked the ball over to me. "Offense or defense?" she asked.

"Um," I said, putting my foot on the ball, "instead of playing football . . . can we go boating?"

"Boating?" Lark asked. "Really?"

"Sure!" I said. "Did you ever row before?"

"Never," Lark admitted.

"Oh, Lark, you have to try it," I said. "Ashley and I went rowing with our school last spring. We had a blast."

Lark looked up and said, "What if it starts raining again? The sky looks pretty grey."

"A little drizzle won't hurt us," I said.

Lark smiled. "Okay. If you really want to. But after that – "

"Football!" I said. "I know."

Lark and I headed down to the lake, where a lifeguard was on duty. He gave us permission to take a rowboat out on the water.

After putting on orange lifejackets, Lark and I pushed a small wooden rowboat into the water. The boat rocked as we carefully stepped in and sat down.

"I'll take the oars first," I said. "Then you can give it a shot."

Lark gripped the sides of the boat as I rowed away from the shore.

"Does your dad like to row?" I asked.

"I think he used to go boating with my grandfather," Lark said. She bit her thumbnail. "But he never took me rowing."

He will soon! I thought with a grin.

"Why don't you take the oars for a while, Lark?" I asked. "You'll get the hang of it."

Lark looked nervous as we carefully switched seats. She sat in the middle and took the oars. I sat at the bow – that's sailor-talk for the front of the boat.

I showed Lark how to grip the oars and dig them into the water at the same time.

"Am I doing it right?" Lark asked as she rowed.

I turned and gulped. Our boat was heading straight toward the diving dock!

"Lark – steer away from the dock," I said.

"How?" Lark cried.

"Pick up your left oar!" I said. "And dig in with your right – "

CRUNCH! Too late. The front of our rowboat got stuck underneath the dock!

"I stink at this." Lark groaned.

"It's no big deal," I said.

We leaned over and tried freeing the boat. It was so wedged in, it didn't budge. And as if things weren't bad enough, it started to rain. Not just a little drizzle, but a sky-opening, cloud-gushing downpour!

The lifeguard started shouting directions at us. Other campers and counselors stood on the shore, watching.

"This is soooo embarrassing!" Lark cried.

It was even more embarrassing when the lifeguard rowed his own boat over to rescue us.

"I don't ever want to see another rowboat in my life," Lark muttered as we were rowed back to shore. "Ever!"

Our feet sloshed in the mud as we walked to Bunk Elvis.

Maybe Lark was right, I thought. *Maybe she and her dad don't have anything in common. . . .*

And maybe I should mind my own beeswax!

Dear Diary,

Most of the bands spent the rainy day playing Rock 'n' Roll bingo. But not Electric Pink. We decided to practise all morning.

"We have to be ready for the Battle of the Bands on Monday," I said. We dodged raindrops on our way to the music building.

"And for *Venus*," Erin added.

Jennifer had to supervise bingo, but she left us her tape recorder so we could hear what we sounded like.

"Let's run through the whole song," I said as we set up in our music room. I plugged in the tape recorder and when we were ready I clicked the record button.

"'Great to know you, great to know you,'" we sang. "'Where would I be if I didn't meet you?'"

Somewhere in the middle of the song there was a knock on the door, and Linda opened it. "Sorry to interrupt, but I cleaned your go-go boots," she said. "They're in the costume cabin if you want them."

"Thank you so much," Phoebe said. She turned to us and said, "Let's grab them before anyone can get to them again."

"Good idea," I said.

We left our instruments and followed Linda to the costume cabin. Our boots were neatly lined up on a table – and they looked clean.

"No more spaghetti and meatballs," Linda said, holding out a boot. "No saucy smell, either. Take a whiff."

The last thing I wanted to do was sniff a boot – even if it *was* my own. "That's okay," I said. "I believe you."

The three of us carried our boots back to the music room. This time we shut them safely inside a cabinet.

"Let's pick up the song from the top," I said.

Erin sat at her keyboard. Phoebe and I lifted our guitars. We both started to strum. But the notes we were playing were totally mixed up!

"Hey!" I said. "My chords are all screwy!"

"So are mine," Phoebe said.

We quickly inspected our guitars.

"Omigosh!" I gasped. "Our strings were all switched!"

Erin rubbed her fingers together. "My keys feel all slimy," she said. "Ewww – someone rubbed butter all over them!"

"Somebody ruined our instruments," Phoebe declared.

The three of us stared at one another. "Venus!" we shouted in unison.

"But how could they switch your strings so fast?" Erin asked. "We were only gone around half an hour."

"Jennifer said that Abigail is great at changing guitar strings," Phoebe said. "And fast, too."

That did it, Diary. Now I was mad!

"I don't care if we *are* snitches," I said. "We're going to tell Stella everything."

We marched to the main building. We knocked on the door of Stella's office. A girl's voice sweetly said, "Come in!"

I opened the door and froze. The girls of Venus were scurrying around Stella's office. Tori was watering Stella's plants. Abigail was refilling the coffeemaker, and Skye was stuffing envelopes.

"What are you doing here?" I asked.

Stella glanced up from her desk. "They just came by to help me around the office," she said. "Isn't that nice?"

"We couldn't think of a better way to spend a rainy day," Skye said with a smile.

"Stella does so much for us," Abigail said. "Isn't it time we did something for her?"

"You guys are the best," Stella said. Then she looked at us. "Now . . . what can I do for you?"

My mouth opened to speak, but nothing came out. Why bother telling Stella about the boots and the instruments? Now *she* thought the girls of Venus were total angels, too!

"It's okay," I said, shaking my head. "It's not important."

Phoebe and Erin shook their heads, too. We filed out of the building. Once outside, I turned to Phoebe and Erin. "I think it's time," I declared.

"Time for what?" Erin asked.

I took a deep breath and said, "Time to *get even*!"

Chapter 10

Saturday

Dear Diary,

Phoebe wanted to switch Venus's sheet music. Erin wanted to crack eggs in their space boots. But I had another idea. . . .

"Let's do something to their precious bubble machine," I said. "That's what they're so proud of."

So last night while everyone was asleep, Phoebe, Erin, and I sneaked out of our bunk. But just as we were about to run to the music building, Phoebe grabbed my arm. "Wait!" she whispered. "There's a counselor on night duty. She's sitting on the porch of Bunk Elton John."

We ducked behind a tree and peeked out. Natalie Berg was sitting under a porch light, reading a magazine.

"How are we going to get past her?" I whispered.

"I have an idea," Erin whispered. She picked up a stone and tossed it into the bushes next to Bunk Elton John. It made a sharp rustling noise.

Natalie jumped up. "Is someone there?" she called.

I held my breath as Natalie walked to the far side of the porch with a flashlight. As soon as she was busy inspecting the bushes, I whispered, "Let's go!"

Twist and Shout

The three of us raced across the campgrounds to the music building. We couldn't go too fast because Erin kept tripping in her pink fuzzy slippers.

Once inside I flipped on the light switch and looked around. Venus's silver space costumes were hanging on a rack. Their instruments were standing against the wall. And their bubble machine was set up on the floor – right where we hoped it would be.

Phoebe picked up a plastic bottle next to the machine. The label read, BUBBLE MACHINE SOLUTION. "This must be the stuff that makes the bubbles," she said.

"And this must be where it goes," I said, opening a small compartment on top of the machine. There was a drop of blue bubble solution still inside.

"Here's the switch," Erin said, pointing to a dial. "Maybe we can turn the bubble machine to High while Venus is practicing."

"We can't switch the machine while they're in here," I said. "They'll see us."

"How else can we pump up the bubbles?" Phoebe asked.

Good question! I paced the room as I thought.

"Mary-Kate and I had a bubble blizzard once," I said. "In our kitchen back in Chicago."

"What happened?" Phoebe asked.

"Our dad goofed." I giggled. "He put liquid dish soap into the dishwasher by mistake. As soon as he turned it on, the whole kitchen was flooded with bubbles."

"Too bad there isn't a dishwasher in this room," Phoebe said, laughing. "We could have done the same thing."

"Hey, wait a minute!" I said. "We can put dishwashing liquid in the bubble machine."

Phoebe smiled and said, "So when they turn it on – "

"Bubble attack!" Erin squealed.

It was the middle of the night, so we tried to not laugh too loud. "It's a great plan," I said. "We just need some dishwashing liquid."

The kitchen was locked, so we waited until the morning.

As everyone filed into the mess hall for breakfast, I turned to Ivy. "Phoebe, Erin, and I would like to practice during breakfast" I said. "We already ate some granola bars in the bunk."

"Okay," Ivy said. "But you'll be missing French toast with cinnamon sugar and maple syrup."

My mouth watered. But the French toast would have to wait. We were on a mission!

Phoebe, Erin, and I ran around the mess hall to the kitchen. We were going to ask the staff if we could borrow some dishwashing liquid, but we didn't have to – there were two bottles of Swishy Dishy on the kitchen windowsill.

"Lemon . . . or antibacterial?" Erin asked.

"Any!" I said.

Erin grabbed the bottle of lemon-scented soap and stuck it under her sweatshirt.

We raced to Venus's practise room. Erin filled the bubble machine with Swishy Dishy – all the way to the top.

"We'd better go," Phoebe whispered. "Breakfast will be over soon."

"But I want to watch when they turn on the bubble machine!" Erin said.

"Okay," I said. "We'll wait in our practise room until we hear Venus come. Then we'll peek through their door."

Phoebe, Erin, and I went to our practise room. We left the door open a crack and listened. It wasn't long before we heard voices in the hall.

"Let's run through the song before Tina gets here," Skye was saying. "We don't need her."

I smiled at my friends. "It's showtime!"

We glanced down the hall to make sure Venus was in their room. We snuck up to the door and peeked through the small glass window.

The girls were already playing. Tori was on drums, Abigail was on bass, and Skye was on electric guitar.

"'Your love is a million light years away,'" they sang. "'But nothing on Earth can stand in our waaaaay!'"

The bubble machine! I thought. *What about the bubble machine?*

I sighed with relief when Abigail switched on the machine with her toe. Only a few bubbles popped out. Until –

WHOOSH! Thick foam gushed out of the machine onto the floor. Soon, the whole room turned into a bubble storm!

"Shut that thing off!" Skye shrieked.

"I did!" Tori screamed. "The bubbles won't stop!"

Phoebe, Erin, and I laughed as the girls tried to fight the out-of-control bubbles.

"It worked," I said. "Our plan worked!"

"What *plan*?" a voice demanded.

Phoebe, Erin, and I spun around. Stella was standing behind us.

Uh-oh! I thought. *We're toast!* And I didn't mean French toast with cinnamon and sugar!

The door swung open, and bubbles poured out. Skye, Tori, and Abigail ran out of the room. Their clothes and hair looked wet and sticky.

Twist and Shout

Skye glared at us. "They did it, Stella!" she said. "They messed with our bubble machine."

"Why, what makes you say that?" Erin asked sweetly.

Skye pointed to the bottle of Swishy Dishy in Erin's hands.

"Oh!" Erin gulped.

"Camp Rock 'n' Roll doesn't stand for pranks," Stella said. "I'm afraid Electric Pink is out of the Battle of the Bands. You're disqualified."

Dear Diary,

When I heard Ashley's news, I was stunned.

"I wish you'd told me what you were planning to do, Ashley," I said. "I would have talked you out of it."

Ashley and I were alone in the bunk. We sat on the floor and leaned against the bed frames.

"Too late now," Ashley said, and sighed. "We blew it."

Lark suddenly ran into the bunk. "They're getting a football game together outside," Lark said. She grabbed my hand and pulled me up. "The teams are called the Rolling Stones and the Supremes."

The three of us ran outside. Campers were already sitting on the grass around the main field.

Ashley found Phoebe and sat next to her. Lark and I ran over to Beverly, the counselor-ref.

"You'll be midfielder for the Stones, Mary-Kate," Beverly said. "Lark, you'll play forward for the Supremes."

Beverly handed out bandannas – red for the Stones, blue for the Supremes. We tied them around our necks.

After the kickoff, Lark excelled as usual. She dribbled the ball like a pro. When the ball was kicked in her direction, she headed it and sent it flying across the field!

"Suuuper!" a voice shouted.

I knew that voice anywhere!

I turned and saw Rodney Beecham. He was wearing a black T-shirt, white drawstring pants – and a huge smile.

What's he doing here? I wondered. *He isn't supposed to come until tomorrow!*

"Owww!" A girl on my team named Kimberly stumbled to the ground, rubbing her calf.

Beverly called a time-out and hurried over. "It's just a cramp," she said. "But you'd better sit it out, Kimberly."

Beverly turned to the campers on the grass. "Who wants to sub for Kim?"

Nobody answered. Until –

"Come on, mates!" Rodney shouted. "Let's show those Supremes we've got game!"

Rodney ran onto the field. He picked up the ball and shouted, "What are we waiting for? Let's play ball!"

Rodney Beecham plays soccer? I thought. *No way!*

Lark looked surprised, too. "Dad?" she said.

"Here you go, love," Rodney said. He shot the ball over to Lark. In a flash, her stunned face turned into her game face, and she kicked the ball way across the field!

"Suuuper!" Rodney cheered again.

You should have been there, Diary. Rodney played an amazing game, and so did Lark. In the end, Lark shot the winning goal kick, and the Supremes won!

"That's my girl!" Rodney shouted. He lifted Lark on his shoulders and paraded her around the field.

"Yaaaay, Lark!" I cheered with everyone else.

Lark had never looked so happy. And I was happy, too. That's because Lark and her dad *do* have something in common, Diary. Something that isn't even in the book.

Football!

Chapter 11

Sunday

Dear Diary,

I can't remember ever being so  bummed out. All the other campers were practising for the Battle of the Bands tomorrow, but not Electric Pink.

Phoebe was on her bed, reading a book of poetry. *Sad* poetry – to match her mood. I lay on my own bed, staring at the ceiling. Erin tried to keep busy by alphabetizing her lip gloss.

"All that hard work," I said. "For nothing."

"It's Venus's fault that we were disqualified, you know," Erin said. "They started it."

"We didn't have to get even," I pointed out.

"Let's just talk to Stella and tell her every rotten thing Venus did to us," Phoebe said.

"We still don't have any proof," I said, shaking my head. "And everyone thinks those girls are angels – including Stella."

The bunk door opened. Jennifer walked inside wearing her GUITAR GODDESS T-shirt, jeans, and a very long face.

"I'm just as upset as you guys," Jennifer said. She held out a cassette tape. "Here. I found this inside my tape recorder."

284

Twist and Shout

I rolled off my bed and took the tape. "It's the recording of our last practice," I said. "The day our guitar strings were switched."

"We must have left it in the tape recorder," Phoebe said.

"Now you can have a souvenir of your band," Jennifer said, forcing a smile. She left the bunk.

"Just trash the tape, Ashley," Erin said. "What good is it now?"

I looked at the tape. The words ELECTRIC PINK were written with a pink marker on the label. "No," I said, shaking my head. "Electric Pink was a great band. We should be proud of our music."

I borrowed Janelle's Walkman and slipped the cassette inside. Then I lay on my bed, put on the earphones, and clicked the green Play button.

Our song "Great to Know You" began to play. For a rehearsal, it sounded pretty good.

Then I heard Linda's voice on the tape. That was when she came into the room to tell us about our boots. I could hear us put down our instruments and leave the room.

We must have forgotten to switch off the tape when we went to the costume cabin, I realized.

Then other voices came on the tape.

"I thought they'd *never* leave!"

"Hurry up, Abigail. Switch the guitar strings while I grease up the keyboard!"

"Tori, give me hand. I'll tell you what to do."

"If this doesn't psych out Electric Pink, I don't know what will."

I sat up straight on my bed. I clicked off the tape recorder and turned to my friends. "You guys," I said. "I think we can go to Stella now!"

Dear Diary,

After the soccer game, Rodney joined Bunk Elvis for lunch. While we ate vegetable lasagna, garlic rolls, and salad, Lark and her dad compared their favorite football stars.

"Joe Stanford bends it better than Mick Linfield," Rodney argued.

"Dad, get real!" Lark said. "Nobody is better than Mick. He rules!"

"Lasagna, Rodney?" Ivy asked, holding out the tray.

Rodney rubbed his hands. "Pass it over here, love!" he said. "Lasagna is my favorite!"

"Really?" I asked across the table. "I thought your favorite dish was macaroni and cheese."

Rodney stuck his finger in his mouth and pretended to gag. "I wouldn't touch macaroni and cheese with a ten-foot cricket bat!" he said. "Who told you it was my favorite?"

"Your book did," I said. "It also said you love hiking. And boating. And – "

"Hate it!" Rodney interrupted. "The woods creep me out. And nothing makes me want to heave more than a rocky boat."

"But you used to row with your dad," Janelle said.

"Dad brought me along to keep the rowboat from tipping," Rodney said. "So he could stand up and fish."

"But," I started to say. "Your book says – "

"Total rubbish!" Rodney said. "It wasn't written by me. The bloke who wrote it made up most of it."

No wonder the book said nothing about football, I thought. *The guy who wrote it didn't have a clue!*

"How did you learn how to play football so well, Rodney?" Ashley asked.

"At the Sneddington School for Boys," Rodney said. "By the time I was thirteen, I was the school champ. Our team won a cabinet full of trophies."

"My team has won trophies, too, Dad," Lark said.

"I'll have to watch you play," Rodney said.

"When you have a concert in Santa Fe?" Lark asked.

"Forget the concert," Rodney declared. "Just tell me when you're playing, and I'm there."

"Really?" Lark asked. "Suuuuper!"

Janelle leaned over to me. "Mission accomplished," she whispered.

I'm sure there's a lot more that Lark and her dad will learn about each other, Diary. But they won't need my help!

Dear Diary,

I know I already wrote you today, Diary. But guess what? Electric Pink went to Stella with the tape. She listened to it, then sent a counselor to bring Venus to her office.

Diary, you should have seen those Venus girls. They looked totally shocked when Stella played them the tape.

"That's not really us!" Skye said. She pointed to Phoebe, Erin, and me. "They disguised their voices!"

"Nice try, Skye," Stella said. "But as I said before, Camp Rock 'n' Roll doesn't stand for pranks. Not only are they immature, they can be dangerous."

"Does that mean we're disqualified, too?" Skye asked.

"No," Stella said.

"What?" I heard myself gasp. How could *we* be disqualified and not Venus?

"I want *both* of your bands to compete in the Battle of the Bands," Stella said.

"You do?" Phoebe asked.

"Why?" Erin asked.

"All of the work here leads up to the Battle of the Bands," Stella said. "You should experience it, too. *But* you'll all have to help the roadies clear the stage and pack up. That means missing the end-of-summer party."

We all thanked Stella. Then we filed out of her office into the hall.

"We're still going to win, you know," Abigail said to us.

"We'll find out tomorrow," I said.

Venus turned and stalked away.

"Tomorrow!" Phoebe gasped.

"Omigosh!" Erin said. "We have to practise!"

And that's why I'd better stop writing, Diary. Wish me luck!

Chapter 12

Monday

Dear Diary,

Lark is still over the moon about her dad. But I'm kind of worried.

Today is the final round of the Battle of the Bands. What if Lark chokes in front of her dad again? It could spoil everything!

I tried not to think about it as we filed into the theater. This time, the place was decorated to the max. Balloons and banners were hanging everywhere. Rock music blasted from speakers as we took our seats.

A bunch of guys in the back of the theatre were setting up huge lights and cameras. They were wearing RODNEY BEECHAM CONCERT TOUR jackets.

That's probably for Rodney's TV special, I thought. The special was going to be filmed tomorrow.

I looked around at the other bands. Everyone was totally stylin' and so were we. Janelle, Lark, and I were dressed in camouflage cargo pants, halter tops, and short combat boots. Lark and I wore camouflage bandannas on our heads. Janelle tied hers around her neck. She wanted to show off the green and pink streaks in her hair.

Twist and Shout

Ashley sat in the second row. She, Phoebe, and Erin were dressed totally sixties, in plastic minidresses, white go-go boots, and big chunky jewelelry shaped like daisies, hearts, even giant dice. Erin wore rose-colored shades with matching lipstick.

Ashley turned and gave me a thumbs-up sign. I gave her one, too. We were good to go!

"This is the moment we've all been waiting for!" Stella shouted onstage. "The Battle of the Bands!"

Everyone clapped, cheered, and stomped their feet.

"Today our judges have been joined by our favorite rocker," Stella announced. "Rodney Beecham!"

Rodney stood up from the judges' table and took a bow.

"As you all know, the focus of this last round is songwriting," Stella said. "And we'll begin with Crush!"

Omigosh! I thought. *We're first.*

I didn't realize how nervous I was until I got onstage. Everything was a big blur until I sat down behind my cans, buckets, and pails. I raised my drumsticks in the air and waited for Janelle to strum her guitar and shout, "One, two, three!"

Gripping my sticks, I exploded with my left arm and matched it with my right.

"'Just like you! Just like you!'" Janelle and I sang.

Lark shook her tambourine with one hand and gripped the mike with the other. As Lark sang, I listened for her voice to shake. It didn't. In fact, she sounded better than she ever had before!

"'It's just like you to make me smile! It's just like you to drive me wild!'" Lark sang.

I glanced at Rodney. He wasn't watching *me* this time. He was watching Lark – with a proud smile on his face!

Janelle played an awesome guitar solo at the end of the song. Then we lined up and took our bows.

"I was feeling the words, Crush," Clarence said. "Rock on with your funky selves!"

"I'm with Clarence," Sophie said. "Your lyrics were fun and fresh. Good job!"

So far, so good! I thought. *But there's still Terrence.*

"Your lyrics were quite good," he said. "I also see that Lark finally chilled out. Well done, Crush."

Stella announced our score. It was an *eight*!

"Do you believe it?" I shrieked backstage.

"That's the highest score we ever got," Lark said.

Janelle gave her guitar a twang. "How cool is that?" she said.

Twist and Shout

"Way cool!" I declared.

You know what's even cooler, Diary? We might even have a chance of winning!

Dear Diary,

Is it possible to have goose bumps on your teeth? Or between your toes? I was never so nervous.

My knees knocked together as I sat in the theatre watching the other bands. The Corral Chicks performed a great country-rock song they wrote together. Stringz didn't sing but they composed a beautiful instrumental.

"I wish we'd go on already," Phoebe whispered. "This waiting is torture!"

The Corral Chicks got a score of seven. Stringz got a six. Terrence said one of the violins sounded like a cat with hair balls. Ouch!

"All-riiiight!" Stella announced. "I think we've been on this planet long enough. How about a trip to Venus?"

Skye, Tori, and Abigail bounced up. They were wearing their silver jumpsuits and matching space boots. Even their faces were painted silver this time.

Skye, Tori, and Abigail sang a song called "Out of This World." The words were really cute. And their bubble machine was back to normal again.

Everyone in the room seemed to like their song. Especially the judges. They gave Venus the highest score yet: a *ten*!

"Ten?" Phoebe squeaked.

"Now we have to get a ten, too," I whispered. "If we want to win."

"But that's a perfect score," Erin whispered.

"We can do it," I whispered back.

Then it was Electric Pink A Go-Go's turn.

I tried not to think about Venus as we climbed up on the stage. Erin sat down behind her keyboard. Phoebe and I stood side by side with our guitars.

"Remember," I murmured. "We can do it."

Erin began the opening melody. As we sang "Great to Know You," I saw mod daisies and hearts flashing on the stage wall. But when Jennifer projected pictures of friends at camp, the audience went wild.

"'Great to know you! Who would have guessed?'" we sang. "'My friendship with you would be the best!'"

Phoebe and I strummed the last few chords of the song. Then it was over. The audience cheered loudly as we bowed.

Twist and Shout

Sophie thought our song was "heartwarming." Clarence said we had a "foot-tapping beat." Even Terrence liked our lyrics. He called them "catchy."

We did it, I thought, squeezing Phoebe's and Erin's hands. *With those responses, we had to get –*

"Nine!" Stella announced. "Electric Pink a Go-Go gets a nine score."

My stomach dropped. I tried not to look, but I saw three faces smirking at us from the audience.

Three *silver* faces!

"Will our counselors tally up the scores of all four rounds?" Stella asked. "Then we can declare a winner."

Phoebe, Erin, and I picked up our instruments and trudged back to our seats.

"It's bad enough losing," Erin muttered. "But did we have to lose to Venus?"

"And now," Stella declared onstage, "the winner of the Battle of the Bands is – "

"We did our best," I said. "What more could we – "

"Electric Pink a Go-Go!" Stella announced.

What?

"Phoebe? Erin?" I asked. "Did she just say – "

"Electric Pink?" Erin squeaked.

"I . . . think . . . so," Phoebe said.

Everyone clapped and cheered. Jennifer ran over and hugged each of us. "You did it," she said. "You won!"

"But . . . how?" I asked.

"Venus had the highest score today," Jennifer said. "But your band had the highest total score."

Phoebe, Erin and I ran onstage. Stella and the judges were waiting for us with three trophies. They were shaped like electric guitars and had inscriptions that read: BEST BAND OF CAMP ROCK 'N' ROLL!

"Go Electric Pink!" I heard Mary-Kate shout.

I smiled as we waved our trophies in the air. Who would have thought things would turn out so awesome? Now we're best band *and* best friends. And that, Diary, is a winning combination!

Chapter 13

Tuesday

Dear Diary,

We won the Battle of the Bands, but we still had to clean up the theatre.

But so did Venus.

"What could be worse than having to clean?" Erin grumbled as she swept the stage.

"Being disqualified?" I said.

"Oh, right!" Erin giggled.

We helped the roadies sweep, move amps, pack equipment, and turn all the seats up. When the work was done, we raced to the rec hall. Luckily, everyone was still partying!

There was a table full of sandwiches, salads, crisps, and jugs of lemonade to drink. Stella had even invited a DJ to spin discs. But the best part wasn't the DJ or the food. It was when Rodney and Lark sang a duet!

"Isn't it awesome?" Mary-Kate asked me. "Rodney is finally paying attention to Lark."

"It *is* awesome," I agreed. "But I think a dad should pay attention to his daughter even if she *doesn't* sing or play football."

Mary-Kate shrugged. "True. But it's a great start."

By the time we got back to Bunk Elvis we were all happy, tired, and little sad, too.

"I'm going to miss Camp Rock 'n' Roll," I said. "I can't believe we're going home on Friday."

"Camp isn't over yet," Ivy said. "We still have three more days of jam sessions."

"*And* we'll get to get to watch Rodney Beecham tape his new TV special," Janelle said. "Featuring Mary-Kate!"

That all happened last night, Diary. And today I'm so tired, I can hardly hold my pen. Which is okay, because I have to stop writing, anyway. Stella just brought Rodney Beecham into our bunk. Maybe he's here to talk to Lark – or to Mary-Kate – about the TV special.

Whatever it is, Diary, we'll find out!

Dear Diary,

As soon as Rodney, Doris, and Stella walked into Bunk Elvis I searched for my drumsticks.

"Is it time to shoot the TV special?" I asked.

Rodney whipped off his shades. "There's been a change of plans, love," he said.

"Rodney wants *Lark* to sing with him in the TV special," Doris said. "Her singing really wowed him yesterday."

Stella smiled at Lark. "You seemed a lot more

comfortable onstage," she said. "We all think you're ready."

Lark's mouth dropped open. She stared at her father. "Are you *sure*, Dad?" she asked.

"Sure, I'm sure!" Rodney said. "You've got your dad's voice. And your mom's good looks!"

Lark smiled, and her eyes lit up. I was happy for her. But worried too.

Does this mean I won't be in the TV special?

It was as if Lark read my mind. "What about Mary-Kate, Dad?" she asked. "You asked her to be in the TV special, too."

"Mary-Kate will still be in the special!" Rodney said. "She'll play her buckets and cans exactly as planned."

Total relief!

"And you," Rodney said, pointing to Janelle. "Your guitar riffs completely brought down the house. How would you like to be in my TV special, too?"

Without a word Janelle fell to her knees and played air guitar.

"I guess that means yes!" Rodney chuckled. "Oh – don't bother learning the words to 'Lively Girl.' I picked a new song that's much better."

"What is it?" I asked.

"It's called," Rodney said, turning to Phoebe, "'Great to Know You!'"

"'Great to Know You?'" Phoebe gasped. "That's *my* song!"

"I really dug it!" Rodney said. "So much that I'd like to sing it, if you don't mind."

"I don't mind!" Phoebe said, her eyes sparkling.

"Just make sure you tell her if you change the lyrics," Erin teased.

Ashley and Erin hugged Phoebe. Rodney pointed to them, too.

"And you girls!" he said. "I could really use some groovy go-go dancers in the TV special. It goes with the theme of my special, 'Getting Mod with Rod!'"

The look on Ashley's face was pure shock. All she could say was, "Omigosh!"

"Our producer has picked a location down by the lake," Doris said. "We'll work on the song all day today, rehearse the TV special tomorrow, and shoot it on Thursday."

"Rock on, girls," Rodney said. Then he, Doris, and Stella walked out of the bunk.

We all stared at one another for what seemed like forever. Then we let out the biggest earsplitting shriek!

Twist and Shout

"Ivy's in the counselor's lounge," Erin said, after we stopped jumping up and down and hugging one another. "Let's tell her the great news!"

We charged out of the bunk. But as the others ran ahead, Ashley and I fell behind.

"You know what, Mary-Kate?" Ashley asked. "I'm glad I let you talk me into Camp Rock 'n' Roll."

"Talk you into it?" I laughed. "Excuse me, but you were packing the minute I showed you the camp brochure!"

We hooked arms and made our way across the campgrounds.

This has been one amazing time, Diary. And it isn't over yet. Not only am I going to play drums for a major rock star on TV, all of my friends are going to be there with me. What could be better than that?

Camp Rock 'n' Roll doesn't only rock – it totally rules!

And so do we!

mary-kateandashley

mary-kateandashley

Sweet 16

(1) *Never Been Kissed*   (0 00 714879 8)
(2) *Wishes and Dreams*   (0 00 714880 1)
(3) *The Perfect Summer*   (0 00 714881 X)

HarperCollins*Entertainment*

PARACHUTE PRESS

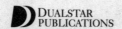
DUALSTAR PUBLICATIONS

mary-kateandashley.com
AOL Keyword: mary-kateandashley